RIFLE PASS

Everybody in town expected Kermit Doyle to pull up stakes after serving his jail term on the trumped-up charges that Skull Bar Ranch had brought against him. For no man could hope to stay alive in Regency with such a powerful outfit against him. And Doyle had other enemies! Hamp Malgren, who would gun him down on sight, and fierce old Jeb Barlow and his sons. But when Doyle emerged from jail he had but one idea—to get his hands on a six-gun and cut down his enemies man by man!

RIFLE PASS

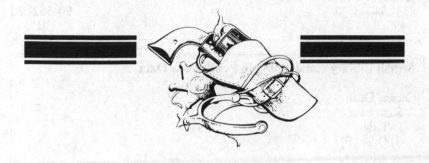

Dean Owen

ATLANTIC LARGE PRINT
Chivers Press, Bath, England.
Curley Publishing, Inc.,
South Yarmouth, Mass., USA.

Library of Congress Cataloging-in-Publication Data

Owen, Dean.
   Rifle pass / Dean Owen.
      p.   cm.—(Atlantic large print)
   ISBN 0–7927–0311–1 (lg. print)
   1. Large type books.   I. Title.
   [PS3565.W53R54   1990]
   813'.54—dc20   90–35270
                                                        CIP

British Library Cataloguing in Publication Data

Owen, Dean
   Rifle pass.
   I. Title
   813'.54 [F]

   ISBN 0–7451–9863–5
   ISBN 0–7451–9875–9 pbk

This Large Print edition is published by Chivers Press, England, and
Curley Publishing, Inc, U.S.A. 1990

Published by arrangement with Donald MacCampbell, Inc

U.K. Hardback ISBN 0 7451 9863 5
U.K. Softback ISBN 0 7451 9875 9
U.S.A. Softback ISBN 0 7927 0311 1

CHAPTER ONE

Not a drop of rain fell during the winter Kermit Doyle spent in the Regency jail, and to the day of his release in the early spring, conditions had not improved. He had heard the anxious talk of the townspeople who gathered in tight little knots on Primrose Street, for the window of his second-floor cell seemed to catch all sound and movement in the town. Out on the Flats, rumor claimed, a man had to ride with a bandanna over his nose, the stench of dead cows was so bad. As with most rumors, Doyle considered this an exaggeration. But the talk did give him something tangible to dwell upon, for his mind was crowded with thoughts of the ugly past and much bitterness darkened his mind.

He stood tall at his cell window, staring across the flat roofs of the dying town, to the hills, shimmering in the heat and beyond, the purple haze of the Rubios. By squinting his hard gray eyes against the sun glare, he could almost see the slot in the mountains that was Rifle Pass. Beyond the pass was Copperjack, the sprawling mine that had once given the town of Regency an excuse for existence. On this side of the pass, in the bleak hills, was what Kermit Doyle had once referred to as his ranch. He turned from the cell window,

1

feeling a raw impatience grip him.

Instinctively he ran the tips of his fingers through the heavy beard that covered the lower half of his face. He had never gotten used to the beard, for prior to coming to Regency he had been smooth-shaven. But to humiliate him further in the jail he had been denied a razor or the services of a barber during his six-month sentence.

'It will soon be over,' he said aloud, a little surprised at the sound of his own voice. 'Then we'll see.'

It was the longest morning he had spent in the cell. As noon passed and Deputy Sol Dinker had not appeared to release him, the bitterness and the solid hatred toward the men who had put him here increased. He thought, They're going to let me sweat. Right up to the last, they're going to make me realize that I'm completely helpless.

The afternoon wore on and it was after three o'clock before Dinker's fat face appeared outside the cell and smiled at Doyle through the bars. There was a well larded look to Dinker. He was thick through the chest and neck; also in the head, Kermit Doyle had decided.

'Getting restless?' Dinker said smugly.

'It's my day to get out of here,' Doyle told him.

'Now, ain't that right,' Dinker said. Already his cotton shirt had darkened from

2

perspiration, for the day was full of the heat of approaching summer. 'But the day don't end till midnight,' Dinker said.

Doyle held himself in. He could feel the blood rush to his head and he longed for an open door between himself and the smiling deputy. But one thing he had learned in the Regency jail—discipline. He could hold his emotions in check and he knew that if this had not been learned he would now be dead. For from the first, they had intended that he should never leave this place alive.

'I've waited six months,' Doyle said evenly. 'I can wait till the day ends at midnight.'

Dinker stood uncertainly a moment, eyeing the prisoner. He seemed disappointed that Doyle would give him no excuse for violence. He took a hitch at his gun rig and turned back to the office, walking stiff-legged because of his fat thighs.

For a long moment after the office door had closed, Doyle stood trembling. Don't let me do some fool thing, he thought. Not on my last day here. For six months I've given them no reason to take a gun. Just one more evening. Then at midnight...

There was one redeeming feature to the Regency jail that Doyle had fully appreciated: the thick walls of handcut stone which tempered the heat of the sun that pushed over the Temple Hills in the morning, touching the Flats and then the town before it dropped into the night pit west of the Colorado. The jail had been built when Regency was King Copper and the city treasury had contained such a surplus that stone masons from Frisco and Denver were imported to work on the two-story building. But like half the town, the jail had outlived its usefulness and was now a monstrosity, only one or two of its twenty cells occupied at a time by a drunk or perhaps a rustler awaiting transfer to the Territorial Prison down at Yuma.

For the rest of the afternoon Doyle sweated out his impatience. Dinker brought him the usual frugal evening meal, forcing him to stand facing the wall, hands clasped behind his neck, while the deputy placed the tray on a stool and backed out and locked the cell door.

Only then was Doyle allowed to touch the food. He ate because it would give him strength; the meals were leftovers from the King Copper Cafe. Once during his stay here he had been violently ill, and Dinker had watched him writhe on the floor, making no move to help him. But in two days Doyle recovered from the effects of the food poisoning. After that he carefully smelled the food and tasted it before eating.

When the meal was over and Dinker had collected the tray, Doyle went to the window. The jail stood on a knoll at the west end of Primrose Street, and when he watched from his second floor cell window, few of the town's activities escaped him.

He knew this was Friday night for he had a clear view of the handsome, big-boned Sid Gunwright, who rode in from the Skull Bar and left his horse at Anse Lipscomb's Livery. Something tightened in Doyle when, through the bars, he saw Gunwright move through the evening shadows to Sabrina Hale's yellow house at the far end of Primrose Street. He saw Gunwright disappear in the poplar grove that surrounded the house. Doyle felt a drop of sweat roll down the back of his neck and he warned himself to caution. The humiliation would soon be over and there were many scores to settle.

At first, Doyle had silently raged at his helplessness on these Friday nights when Gunwright rode in from the ranch. He would stand at the cell window, watching the lamplighted windows of Sabrina's house go dark. Much later, when the horses at the rack in front of Pellman's Saloon had thinned out, Doyle would watch Gunwright walk along the street. The rancher would stand on the porch of Pellman's, his heavy figure in the full glow of the kerosene lantern above the door. Gunwright would light one of his custom-made cigars, letting the match flare touch his bland features so there could be no mistake in identity.

Tonight was no exception. He saw

5

Gunwright light his cigar, then turn into Pellman's for a late drink or a hand of poker.

Later that night a few of Gunwright's Skull bar crew rode in for a little helling. From his cell window Doyle saw some of them turn down Chavez Alley where the curtained windows of Mom Lanfield's place beckoned. When the door of the place had closed and the squeals of welcome from the girls subsided, Doyle saw a lone figure in the street in front of Pellman's; it was the man he should have killed six months ago.

Hamp Malgren staggered a little as he shook a fist at the jail. 'I'll be waiting for you, Doyle!' he shouted drunkenly. The Skull Bar rider still held his left arm at an awkward angle, Doyle observed; his bullet must have clipped a nerve or a muscle in Malgren's arm.

Little would have been said of that shooting six months ago, had it not been for the fact that at the moment Doyle fired, Malgren tripped over a stone. The Skull Bar man's big body had been turned so that the bullet, instead of catching him in the chest as Doyle intended, had entered his shoulder from the back. Because Malgren was a Gunwright rider, and because of Gunwright's political power, a jury had taken it upon themselves to believe Malgren's version of what had happened. They agreed that Doyle had shot Hamp Malgren in the back.

At midnight, Tom Joplin, the lank night

deputy, shuffled down the corridor to grin crookedly through the bars of the cell door. He was a tobacco chewer, and if anything he was a shade meaner than his partner, Sol Dinker. Once during his stay here Doyle had seen Joplin put on his horse-shoe ring, made of a nail, worn so the two ends were crossed in front of the finger, and use it on a drunk who had been sick on the stone cell floor. Blood splotched the floor when Joplin finished and the man's face was horribly cut.

Joplin had turned to Doyle, grinning. 'You don't like what I done to that fella?' he said softly. 'Then speak up.'

For a moment Doyle had been tempted to cry out against this brutality. But his eyes fell to the bloodied ring on the deputy's finger. And Joplin wore a gun and there was a sawed-off shotgun leaning against the corridor wall. He knew what was going on in Joplin's mind: manacle him to the bars, work him over with the ring, then shoot him. And the record would say: Attempted Escape.

Tonight Joplin, chewing tobacco, said, 'I ain't yet got a release from the sheriff to turn you loose.' He seemed almost concerned about it and Doyle was instantly on his guard. 'So you'll have to wait till morning,' Joplin finished.

Doyle clenched his fists. 'I'll wait.'

Joplin grinned and some of the tobacco juice angled across his chin. 'I just know you'll wait.' Then he spat expertly through the bars, throwing a brown smear of tobacco juice across the floor of Doyle's cell.

For a moment the two men stared at each other through the bars. Only by the bleakness in Doyle's blue eyes could a man tell that he had been outwardly affected by this indecency.

Joplin drawled, 'Better tidy up. Wouldn't want to see you get extra time for having a dirty cell.'

Doyle made no reply. He just looked—and fought down an urge to reach through the bars and catch Joplin's thin neck in his hands.

Joplin's lips were flat against his teeth, stained from the tobacco. 'Did I hear you cuss me?' he murmured.

Doyle shook his head and could not resist an urge to say, 'You didn't earn your money, did you?' It was a reckless thing to do and the moment he spoke he knew it could still give Joplin the excuse he needed. But the accusation was in the open now.

'What money you talking about?' Joplin said, his thick brows angling in above the bridge of his sharp nose.

'The money Sid Gunwright gave you and Dinker to get me mad enough to do some crazy fool thing. So you'd have an excuse to shoot me.'

For a moment Joplin seemed confused, as

8

if unable to cope with so blunt a statement. Then he stepped close to the cell and laid tongue to every vile word one man can call another. Doyle's lips whitened, but he kept his mouth shut.

When Joplin finally ran out of steam, he spat again on the cell floor and stomped back to his office. Doyle wiped up the mess of tobacco juice with a rag he kept for the purpose.

Unable to sleep, he stepped to the windows. A few lights still glowed along Primrose Street, but Copperjack Street, named for the mine which had boomed Regency, was dark. Formerly it had been the main business block, but the buildings that fronted it were now boarded up and falling slowly to ruin under the desert sun. There was an air of decay about the town as if the shutting off of the Copperjack had brought on a creeping death. The trickle of ore now seeping from the mine could not satisfy those who had lived grandly in the boom days. And such were Sid Gunwright and Sabrina Hale.

There was a restlessness in the air so tangible it could be registered by the senses. Kermit Doyle had felt it before, once on the eve of an attack at a place called Manassas. And now, standing in his cell in the stillness that comes before dawn, he again experienced a fluttering of his nerves, knowing with a certainty that men now sleeping out there in

9

the darkness would experience sudden and shocking death.

The thought left him a little sick as he realized his own part in this.

Finally he went to sleep.

CHAPTER TWO

When the early sun threw its shadowed patterns on the cell floor, Kermit Doyle was told to make himself ready for his release. It was Joplin who brought the message and the lank deputy seemed almost unhappy about it. Doyle washed his face and ran a comb through his uncut brown hair. He combed his beard, staring at his reflection in a wedge of mirror he had fastened to the wall. The wide-spaced blue eyes looked out above the forested planes of his face. His mouth was almost hidden by the blend of beard and mustache.

Joplin walked behind him down the long corridor, past the empty cells with doors ajar that had once held the lawless of Regency. The other deputy, Sol Dinker, stood with heavy shoulders against the office wall, arms folded across his chest.

Doyle was surprised to see Sheriff Matt Conodine seated at the desk. It meant that the sheriff had ridden fifty miles to be on hand for the occasion of Doyle's release.

'I'm honored, Sheriff,' Doyle said tightly. He neither liked or disliked Conodine. The man was of medium height, slightly bald, Perpetually harassed by the increasing pressure of his job, Conodine looked older than he had six months ago when he first locked Doyle in his cell. There was a lot more gray in the sheriff's hair, and the lines that flanked his small mouth were deeper.

'I didn't come all the way over here to honor you,' the sheriff said crisply. 'It was to give you some advice.'

'I'll take your advice,' Doyle said.

The sheriff gave him a sharp look. 'It'll be the first time anybody could tell you anything.'

'I'm agreeable,' Doyle said with a faint smile, 'because I'm not out of here yet.'

'You're right about that, Doyle,' Conodine said, and jabbed his thumbs into his vest pocket. 'You've been in this country nearly a year,' he said, 'and for most of that time we've had trouble, or threats of it.'

'Discounting the six months I spent in your jail,' Doyle reminded him.

'Yeah.' Conodine leveled a forefinger at him. 'If you've got any sense at all, Doyle, you've learned your lesson.'

Doyle watched the man draw deeply on a cigar, and he sniffed the aroma of good Havana tobacco. His eyes strayed to

11

Conodine's desk and the narrow paper band that had been removed from the cigar. Even from this distance Doyle could read the initials, SG, stamped in small gold letters on the paper band.

From the desk drawer the sheriff removed a blackened shell belt, the loops filled with cartridges, and the gun and holster. Joplin and Dinker looked on with tight amusement when Doyle buckled on the harness. It gave a man confidence, Doyle thought, to feel the weight of a gun once again. Then he caught the smiles on the faces of the two deputies and knew something was wrong. He drew the gun. Its muzzle had been spiked with a piece of rusting iron.

He had to wait a moment before speaking. But he could not let this matter of the gun go unnoticed. A man had his pride.

He extended the ruined gun, saying, 'It was in good shape when I checked in here, Sheriff.'

Sheriff Conodine's skull reddened, the portion that Doyle could see in front of his tipped-back hat. 'I had nothing to do with the gun,' Conodine said, and shifted uneasily in his chair. Then a sudden anger seemed to possess him as if this business has pushed him too far. 'Don't forget it's the same gun you used on a man when his back was turned.'

'I'd do it again,' Doyle said.

Conodine's face deepened in color.

'Consider yourself lucky, Doyle. If Malgren had died, you'd have been hanged months ago.'

Doyle swallowed. 'You know what Malgren was doing and why I shot him,' he said.

'Your word,' Conodine muttered, 'and the word of Ellie Barlow.'

From the street below came the faint sounds of a wagon moving over the ruts, the pound of a team, then silence. A cloud of yellow dust drifted through the barred window to remind a man that for eleven months there had been no rain.

Doyle's shoulders stiffened. 'Does drawing pay from the Skull Bar give a man the right to have his way with a woman?'

'Course it don't,' Conodine said, stirring again in his chair. Then he added, 'But those hill women aren't very long on morals—' The sheriff's voice trailed off. Although he was sheriff and had two deputies at his elbow and this was his jail, something in Doyle's eyes made him unwilling to finish the sentence. 'Sid Gunwright or his men,' he added lamely, 'get no special privileges around here.'

Doyle did not laugh, although the urge was in him, and neither did the thin coldness alter in his gaze. 'You smoke a good brand of cigars, Sheriff,' he said softly, and jerked his head at the cigar band which lay on the desk.

Conodine's cheeks flushed. 'So Gunwright

gave me a cigar! What of it?' He clenched his fists and glared up at this tall, quiet man. 'You owe me something, Doyle.'

'What do I owe you?'

'Probably your life.' He leveled the forefinger again. 'I could have released you last night. Know why I didn't?'

'You tell me.'

'Because the town was full of Skull Bar men. I got Gunwright to agree to move them to Dutchman's Flats.' The sheriff got to his feet and banged a fist down on the desk. 'This is your chance to get out—for good!'

Doyle looked at him a moment, then said, 'You forget something. I'm a property owner. I'm not going to ride out and leave a ranch.'

'See Loren Pellman,' the sheriff said. 'He has a message for you concerning your property.' With shaking hands Conodine ripped open an envelope and handed Doyle the fourteen dollars he'd had in his possession the night the posse ran him down at his place out in the Temple Hills.

Doyle stuffed the money into his pants pocket. 'Am I free to go?' He shifted his gaze to Dinker and Joplin who regarded him thinly from their positions against the wall.

The sheriff said, 'Don't forget to see Pellman on your way out.' Then he pursed his lips. 'Gunwright is going to be generous, considering that you shot one of his men.'

Doyle laid the ruined gun on the desk.

'Maybe you can use this for a paper weight,' he said quietly, and stepped out the door.

He went down the stone stairs and past the courtroom where he had been tried and convicted. And seeing the empty room through a side window, he could not help but remember how Ellie Barlow had looked in the witness chair, her coppery hair brushed so it glistened in the sunlight, her face dead white.

He remembered the snickers from the crowd when the prosecutor made reference to a girl who would go off in the brush with a man. But Ellie had steadfastly denied this in a calm, controlled voice. She was young, not yet twenty, and when the trial was over some of the women folks said it was a shame that her name had been blackened for all time and that probably no man in his right senses would ever marry her now. There was a place for such girls, the whispered female voices said, and referred to Mom Lanfield's establishment at the far end of Chavez Alley.

And because the Barlow name had been sullied, old Jeb and his two tough sons, Dave and Curt, spread the blame equally between two men: Hamp Malgren and Kermit Doyle. The Barlows had openly made their brag that one day, when the sign was right, they'd ride down out of the Temple Hills and permanently erase both marks against the name of Barlow.

Outside on the walk Doyle breathed deeply

15

of the air that was warm and faintly tinged with the acrid odor of dryness that lay over the town. It was the same air he had breathed through his cell window for six months, but today it seemed fresher and there was the smell of freedom in it.

When he crossed the street, bone-dry dust swirled up around his boots. He stomped across the narrow porch of Pellman's, looking at the kerosene lantern above the door, unlighted now in the day's glare. He thought of Gunwright standing on this porch, letting the yellow glow wash over him so that his face was visible to the man who had watched in helpless rage from the second floor of the jail. Gunwright, who had come along this walk from a darkened yellow house and from Sabrina Hale.

Doyle entered the saloon, surprised that Loren Pellman was behind his own bar at this early hour. Pellman was a plump, red-faced man, owner of the last saloon in Regency. A man who had seen eighteen competitors go to the wall when the Copperjack all but closed down operations. He extended a soft hand for Doyle to shake.

'I figured you'd want a drink, Kermit,' Pellman said, a little uneasily, 'so I got up early to serve you myself.'

Doyle stiffened at the use of his first name. It was the first time in six months it had been used. Although Pellman had not spoken out

16

against the jury's verdict, six months ago, Doyle had always sensed that the saloon man was secretly displeased.

He took the drink Pellman offered, holding the shot glass in his hand a moment, enjoying the touch of the glass against his flesh. 'Conodine said you have a message for me, Loren,' Doyle murmured.

Pellman frowned and color crept across his moon face. 'Was that the only reason you dropped by?' he asked mildly. 'I'd hate to think that an old customer would leave our country without stopping by.'

Doyle regarded the barkeep a moment, then said, 'I don't remember saying I was going to leave town.' He saw that Pellman's mouth had sprung open in surprise. Doyle took the drink, finding pleasure in the warmth the liquor spread through him.

'Don't joke about it, Kermit,' Pellman said seriously. He wore a clean white shirt that already showed dark rings of perspiration, for the full heat of the day was beginning to bear down. 'You're not fool enough to stay around here.'

'Any reason why I shouldn't?'

Pellman chewed a full lower lip. 'For one thing, there's Hamp Malgren. He's got a stiff arm. He's not going to forget that you gave it to him.'

'I didn't think he'd be the kind to forget it,' Doyle said. He refused a second drink

17

because he had been six months without whisky. His stomach felt comfortable from the prime bourbon Pellman had poured. It reminded him of the good things he had missed. The easy talk with friends, a good cigar, a drink. And the soft arms of Sabrina Hale.

Pellman had reluctantly picked up a check and a folded paper from the back bar and laid it in front of Doyle. 'Remember this,' Pellman said, lowering his voice—although there was no need because the place was empty save for the two of them—'I'm not taking sides. But Gunwright asked me to do him a favor.'

'And you couldn't refuse,' Doyle said.

'Not and stay in business here,' Pellman said quickly.

'I understand, Loren.'

Pellman's head was bald and it glistened wetly. He dried it with dabs of a bandanna handkerchief against the pink, hairless flesh. 'It's a check for your Cross L,' Pellman said, 'and a quit claim deed for you to sign.'

'After six months,' Doyle said, 'a man could forget how to sign his name.'

'Don't make light of this, Kermit.'

Doyle glanced at the check, seeing Gunwright's bold signature. The amount was for eight hundred dollars. Doyle shut his eyes, visualizing the windows of the yellow house in the poplar grove going dark of a

18

Friday night.

'Take the check, Kermit,' Pellman urged. 'You're a nice fella. I like you. There's no sense in you getting dead for some stubborn pride.'

'I knew the risks when I settled here,' Doyle reminded him.

Pellman nodded soberly. 'But you're a newcomer. You've been around here a year, and a lot of us in town were hoping you could make a go of the old Tilson place. But right away you got in bad. You stepped on Gunwright's toes and it hurt.' Pellman stopped, obviously embarrassed, and wiped his head again with the bandanna. 'You stole his girl. A man doesn't hold still for that, Kermit.'

Doyle gave a bitter laugh. 'She's back now, where she belonged all the time,' he said grimly. 'With Gunwright.'

'Now I wouldn't be too sure about that,' Pellman said.

'If you're ever in jail, Loren,' Doyle said, 'try and get on the second floor. You'd be surprised at the things you can see.'

Pellman lowered his eyes and Doyle thought, he knows about Gunwright and Sabrina. The whole town knows.

'Look, it isn't Sabrina that will turn Gunwright on you this time,' Pellman said patiently. 'It's water. Since you've been in jail we've had no rain. There's water in the hills,

19

though. And with your place Gunwright will have a toehold there.'

'If I back out now,' Doyle said, a trace of bitterness in his voice, 'I'll be deserting my good friends, the hill crowd.'

'Let the hill bunch settle their own affairs.'

Doyle said, fingering the check, 'I don't really know, Loren.'

'You're in the middle. The Barlows practically run the hill ranchers and they hate you because of Ellie's name being dragged in the mud.'

'I saved her from Hamp Malgren,' Doyle said.

'So you did,' Pellman agreed. 'But Jeb Barlow is a good hater and so are his two boys. I'd say it's a toss-up whether they hate you or Malgren the most.'

Doyle was silent a moment. It was no secret that the Barlows hated him because of Ellie. And he found himself wondering how she felt about him. The same way, probably. He remembered how she had walked past him, without glancing his way, her head held high, the day the verdict was returned by the jury.

Pellman was talking again about the troubles of a country that had nearly abandoned cattle, living off the lush profits of the Copperjack. Hardly a man, among the old timers, had not bought stock when it was first offered. Pellman had his own reminder of the

20

boom days, a gold inlaid chandelier hanging above the sawdust-strewn floor. It had gathered dust as had most of the town and now it was tarnished. The chandelier had come from New Orleans and Chicago bankers had sat under it.

In the family room out back—used now for storage or card games—banquets had been given, and there were well-dressed ladies with plumes in their hair, the swish of silken skirts, the sparkle of gentlemen's diamond studs. And there had been an orchestra, musicians wearing dress suits with starched white shirts, violins and cellos.

Pellman liked to reminisce about the first time Sabrina had tasted champagne. She was seventeen and her father had brought a prominent financier from San Francisco to stay at the big yellow house at the end of Primrose Street. Sabrina had partaken of the champagne. She had wildly kicked off her shoes, climbed upon a table and danced. She kicked her feet high into the air and some men present, who had been to Paris, said it was better than the can-can.

And probably it was, because Sabrina Hale, beautiful daughter of the wealthiest man in Regency, had come wholly unprepared for such a display. Her father had ordered her down, his face red from embarrassment. But the incident was soon forgotten, for those were the heady, intoxicated days of easy living in Regency. The town where the well would never run dry. But it had. And many were hurt by it.

'You've got no chance here, Kermit,' Pellman said. 'I know this country. I've known Sid Gunwright since he was eight years old and used to drive his Shetland pony team down Primrose Street and set every horse at the racks to pitching.'

Pellman was a realist in a hard country where only a realist could survive. It was no place for a two-bit cattleman who had come here with his dreams. Impractical dreams, as most dreams are. Still...

'They ruined my gun at the jail, Loren. I could use one.'

Pellman's face flushed. 'Don't ask me, Kermit. Please.'

Doyle stiffened, then the tautness went out of his shoulders. After all Pellman was in the middle.

'If I decide to take Gunwright's offer,' Doyle said, 'I'll be back tomorrow.'

He started for the door. Pellman's voice followed him. 'I'd make it sooner than that, Kermit. Gunwright has sent his boys to Dutchman's Flats. Whether he can keep them there or not is another matter.' Pellman came around the end of his bar, worry touching his perspiring face. 'Hamp Malgren is a dangerous man—'

'So am I, when I'm pushed too far.'

22

Pellman hesitated, a forlorn fat man, while Doyle watched him from the door. 'I'll tell you one thing, Kermit,' he said finally. 'I believe your story about what happened between Ellie Barlow and Malgren.' His voice was indignant as he added, 'If I was Jeb Barlow and Ellie was my daughter, I'd hunt Malgren down like a snake and kill him.'

CHAPTER THREE

Early that morning, just before sunup, Hamp Malgren cautiously pushed aside his blanket and glanced around the shadowed Skull Bar cow camp at Dutchman's Flats. He could see the silhouette of the chuck wagon, and Skip Harlow shoving the camp roustabout toward a stack of cut wood for the breakfast fire. Malgren hastily rolled up his blanket, careful to make no noise. Scattered about on the ground were a dozen sleeping figures. Malgren picked up the saddle he had been using for a pillow and moved across the ground. In order to get to his horse, he would have to pass the chuck wagon and that gimlet-eyed old cook, Skip Harlow, would spot him sure.

Malgren made up his mind quickly as the roustabout threw wood on the breakfast fire. Beyond the chuck wagon he could see the

23

three-hundred odd head of Skull Bar cows that Gunwright figured to push into the Temple Hills.

Skip Harlow saw him and Malgren laid a finger across his lips to indicate that he wanted silence. Harlow looked at him with obvious distaste. Harlow had been with Skull Bar since even before Gunwright's daddy had brought home that fancy English woman as his bride. She was a good-looking woman, Harlow had to admit, and she put up with old man Gunwright's drinking and his nights at Mom Lanfield's in Regency. But the plague struck Regency and she died when Sid Gunwright was twelve. Even though Harlow did not agree with everything Gunwright did, he stayed on in memory of the old man, who had come here with a Texas running iron in his gear and four hundred head of cows that had been driven hard and far. In those days the Utes were in this country, and old man Gunwright had expanded his boundaries. Some said there was a dead Ute for every acre of Skull Bar land.

Skip Harlow wore a frock coat, green from age, over his cheap cotton shirt. Old man Gunwright had given him the coat once when they had gone to town on a drunk. Old man Gunwright had been forced to take stock in Copperjack when the mine first opened, because his wife's British cousin had been superintendent. It made him rich, but did not

24

change his mannerisms. He branded cows in a hundred dollar Frisco suit and had the 'boss wagon' constructed for luxury living in the cow camps. His son, Sid, slept in it now; the wagon was over behind the remuda, so heavy it took a team of six mules to pull it.

Harlow surveyed Malgren sourly. 'Boss said nobody's to leave camp,' the old cook told him, and let his gaze slide to the saddle and blanket the rider carried.

'I'm supposed to help them new Texans by showin' 'em around,' Malgren lied. He had hit upon the three Texans who had arrived in camp, as a likely excuse. The men had asked for riding jobs and Gunwright had hired them. Probably more for the guns they wore than from any ability with cattle.

Harlow kept on pounding out biscuit dough. He thought of calling Clyde Fengean, the short-legged Skull Bar foreman, who lay sleeping some distance away. But Fengean was short-tempered enough as it was, so Harlow decided to accept Malgren's story.

Still, the old cook could not resist one perversity. 'Hear that Kermit Doyle gets out of jail today,' Harlow said, wiping flour from his cheek and giving Malgren a slanted look.

He saw the big, dark rider stiffen. Malgren was handsome in a brutal sort of way, the kind of a man some women might find pleasing to the eye. A braggart and a heavy drinker, Malgren. But he was good with cattle and he would fight for the Skull Bar.

Malgren said carefully, 'Doyle won't hang around this country. The boss is giving him eight hundred dollars for the Cross L.'

Harlow pounded the biscuit dough with relish, finding a new way to twist the knife in Malgren. 'Yeah, but the Barlows ain't leaving. Hear they're going to get you, Hamp, if it takes twenty years.'

Malgren turned on the old cook, his face livid. 'You'd like that, wouldn't you?'

There was no fear in Skip Harlow. He was a Skull Bar man, despite his sixty-three years, and he had come up from the Big Bend with old man Gunwright and four hundred head of Mexican cattle. He had shot out the lights in Pellman's one night with the old man at his side, and twenty toughs from a road-building crew ready to jump them with mattock handles. He had seen three men hanged on Skull Bar land, and a dozen or more others shot and buried in unmarked graves. He was old and tired, and the piece of Mexican lead in his right leg pained like hell sometimes. But he reckoned it wouldn't be too long before he'd be hunting up the old man to swap yarns about the days when a woman could ride unmolested across Skull Bar and a man like Hamp Malgren would have died for sure, but neither quickly nor easily.

Skip Harlow picked up a long-bladed butcher knife, and while the roustabout

26

looked on, wide-eyed, he touched the front of Malgren's chest with the sharp point. 'If I had a daughter and she come home with her clothes tore off because of the likes of you—'

Malgren's left hand knocked the knife from Harlow's fingers. His right hand closed around the old man's throat and he lifted him, so that Harlow's feet left the ground. He held him that way for a moment, then let him drop. Harlow crumpled up at the edge of the fire, and it was many minutes after Malgren had roped a horse, saddled it and ridden west, that color came back in Skip Harlow's face.

Malgren, once he was away from the riders on night trick, left the herd at a gallop. He rode toward Regency, and soon the rising sun warmed his back. In him was a fierce exultation. He spurred the horse cruelly across the brushy flats. His cousin was Anse Lipscomb who ran the livery in Regency. And Kermit Doyle would have to go to the stable for his horse before he left town...

        ★   ★   ★

When Doyle left Pellman's in the morning heat and glare, he picked his way over the warped planks of the walk. Twenty miles to the north he could see the Temple Hills rising hot and blue against the harsh dome of the sky. By squinting his eyes he could almost

27

make out Rifle Pass, which was only a pistol shot from the front porch of the ranch house he had not seen in six months. He passed Copperjack Street, looking down the lonely thoroughfare with its abandoned buildings. Boys bent on mischief had broken out most of the windows and the rest were boarded up.

He saw signs: New Orleans House—Mme. Devereaux, Milliner—Ramson's, Attire for the Gentleman. Incongruous now, with weeds choking the alleys, and the store fronts as dead as those who attempted to transplant a dream to this bleak country. A dream of dinner by candlelight, fine Irish linen and the best silver. One of the few who had accepted the broken dream with grace, Doyle had heard, was Mom Lanfield. She had the parlor of her establishment papered with Copperjack stock certificates.

He crossed Copperjack Street, heading for Anse Lipscomb's Livery, and saw a familiar figure. Sabrina Hale usually didn't rise until noon, so he was surprised to see her coming toward him. He stopped short in the dust, aware of a wild beating of his pulse. He hated himself for this betrayal of his emotions, for he felt nothing but disgust toward her.

He studied her as she moved along the street, too casual in her window shopping. There was something regal in her carriage, as if she were the only living holdover from the moneyed days of Regency; the only human

28

being here who looked as if he or she might have been a part of those days.

There was an air of aristocracy about Sabrina. It was in the lift of her chin, her square shoulders and straight back. The dress she wore of some clinging blue fabric made him acutely aware that the body it sought to cover was so completely feminine. She paused halfway down the block to peer in the window of the emporium, but he sensed that she watched him from the corners of her eyes.

He stepped up, removing his hat. He stood there with a full beard and uncut hair, still smelling of the jail.

She appeared surprised to see him, and her fine dark brows arched above her hazel eyes. 'How nice, Kermit,' she said in her deep and pleasing voice.

He caught the scent of the dark hair that coiled loosely on her head. It was on such a morning a year ago, he remembered bitterly, that he had come through this town intending to push on to California after he sold his hundred and fifty head of beef to the Copperjack Mine. But two things forced his hand. The mine was nearly closed down, and the creditors who had taken over the operation refused to acknowledge the beef contract Doyle had signed with the Copperjack rep in Denver. And he had seen Sabrina on the walk, standing just about where she was now. He had moved his horse to the edge of the walk and smiled and doffed his dusty hat.

Something about him had caught her interest. She smiled and that was enough. Instead of taking his dreams to California, he settled for the Temple Hills, close enough so he could see her once a week.

Dire threats had come from Skull Bar, for it was common knowledge that Sabrina had been promised to Sid Gunwright. But Doyle was a man in love. He and Sabrina had been close, with the promise of marriage between them—until that shooting of Hamp Malgren six months ago.

'You look well, Kermit,' she said, and smiled warmly. She twirled the parasol she carried to keep the sun from her pale, finely-featured face.

'It's been a long time, Sabrina,' he said, and stared deliberately in the direction of the jail at the east end of town.

She flushed. 'There are gossips in this town,' she said, smiling again so that he could see the dimple in her right cheek. 'That's why I didn't visit you.'

'Would that have been a tragedy?' he demanded. 'After all, unless my memory has gone back on me, we were running away to be married the night I was arrested.'

For a moment he thought he saw a faint regret in the depths of her hazel eyes. Then it was gone. 'That's what I wanted to see you

30

about, Kermit.' When talking to a man, she always stood with her back slightly arched as if consciously increasing the pressure of her breasts against the front of her dress. She peered up and down the deserted street as if to make sure they were not observed. 'I had brought my trunk out to your place the night we were to leave, remember?' She lowered her eyes. 'It might be embarrassing if it should be found.'

'Why?'

She stiffened. 'It's full of my clothes. Isn't that reason enough?'

He smiled coldly. 'I'll see if it's still at the Cross L,' he told her.

She nodded her dark head in thanks. 'I thought you might destroy it when you stop by to pick up your things.'

She started to turn away, but his voice stopped her. 'You think I'm selling out to Gunwright?' Doyle said.

She seemed surprised. 'I understood you were.'

'I didn't have much when I came into this country,' he reminded her. 'I don't like leaving with less.' He looked at her levelly. She had a magnificent body and a beautiful face to match. He had noticed both that day he first came through Regency. They had prompted him to settle on the old Tilson place at the foot of Rifle Pass.

Suddenly she slipped the glove from her

31

right hand, extending the hand to him. He clasped it in his own, conscious of the warmth of her skin, the slight intimate pressure of her fingers.

'Burn the trunk, Kermit,' she said pleasantly, 'and whatever it contains.' She tilted her dark head to one side. 'Do it for me.'

Even now he couldn't believe what his eyes had seen nights from his cell window. She seemed completely guileless. Yet she was twenty-two and so very wise.

She withdrew her hand and pulled on her glove. He said wickedly, 'I haven't been near a woman for six months. Better keep your windows locked.'

Her hazel eyes glinted and she tugged angrily at the glove. 'Vulgarity isn't becoming to you, Kermit.'

'I forgot,' he said. 'Before I went to jail I didn't climb in through your windows. I used the front door.'

'Oh—' She stamped her foot and he saw her biting her lip. She wanted to revile him, but that secret matter lay between them. That trunk full of clothes at the Cross L.

He touched his hat brim and turned in at Link Johnson's hardware. Through the window he saw Sabrina lifting her skirts against the dust of Primrose Street as she crossed to the opposite walk, her stride stiff with anger.

In the odors of kerosene and leather and the earthy smell of iron utensils he found a certain comfort. He turned, old man Johnson watching him uncertainly over the square tops of his spectacles. Then Link Johnson rubbed the palm of his right hand on his leather apron, and extended the hand to Doyle.

'Good to see you, Kermit.'

Johnson was a tall, fleshless man, a little stooped at the shoulders. He nervously fiddled with some account books on the counter. 'Something I can do for you, Kermit?'

'I've got fourteen dollars, Link,' Doyle said. 'What kind of a gun will it buy?'

Johnson rubbed his chin and looked pained. 'Sheriff Conodine spread the word he'd appreciate it if you left town with an empty holster.'

'Was it the sheriff, or was it Sid Gunwright who gave you the order?'

The flush on Johnson's face spread upward to the roots of his graying head. 'You got to remember, since the Copperjack is near closed down,' he said, 'I get most of my business from Skull Bar.'

'I know.'

There was sympathy in Doyle's voice and it touched the merchant. Johnson lifted his hands, let them fall in a gesture of helplessness. 'Oh, hell, Kermit. I don't like this, but if I sell you a gun I'm whipped.' He banged a bony fist on the counter. 'In fact, I'd *give* you a gun if I could.' Doyle looked grim and pocketed the money he had withdrawn. 'Forget it, Link,' he said, and turned for the door.

But it was murder to turn a man loose in this country without a gun. Doubly so when there was Hamp Malgren on one side of the fence, the three Barlows on the other. Johnson caught up with him.

'Things ain't the same since they locked you up, Kermit,' he said. 'The hill bunch don't hardly ever come to Regency no more. And the Barlows ain't been here in three months.' Johnson gave him a grim look. 'But I heard talk that they might ride in today.'

Doyle frowned. 'That's possible,' he admitted. 'They probably know I got out today.'

'That's what I mean,' Johnson said. 'I s'pose you know this country is set to blow up in our faces.'

Doyle nodded. 'Water level in the basin has dropped.'

'Gunwright's got only one well left,' Johnson went on. 'And from what I hear it ain't pumping much.' He touched Doyle's arm. 'Take Gunwright's offer and clear out while you got the chance.'

'I'm giving it a lot of thought,' Doyle said.

'Gunwright's set to move into the hills,'

Johnson warned. 'There's going to be a lot of boys buried out in the brush before this is over.'

'You ought to get in the undertaking business, Link. And if you do, you'll soon learn that every man looks the same when he's nailed up in a pine box.'

Johnson looked shocked. 'You're not thinking of bucking the Skull Bar, are you?'

Doyle shrugged.

'If you do,' Johnson said, 'you'll fight them alone.'

'Yeah, I know.'

'And while you're looking for Gunwright, you better not turn your back on the Barlows.'

'You might give Gunwright a little of the same warning, Link,' Doyle said, 'before he turns this country into a blood bath.'

Johnson looked helplessly down at his hand. 'I'd tell him if I had the nerve.'

Doyle straightened his shoulders. 'Nobody can tell Gunwright anything,' he said. 'But I suppose you people around here know that already.'

'That we do, Kermit,' Johnson murmured, and watched him step to the door. He then added what he considered a hopeless bit of advice: 'Take care of yourself.'

CHAPTER FOUR

When Kermit Doyle started for Lipscomb's Livery at the east end of town, he became aware that men were drifting out of doorways. By the time he reached the end of the walk a sizable crowd was trailing along in his wake. A man made some remark that Doyle could not hear. A ripple of laughter moved through the ranks of those who followed him.

He could not blame them too much, he supposed. For the most part they were tradesmen, of a cut below Link Johnson and Pellman. They depended on the good will of the Skull Bar for their livelihood. And Doyle sensed what was on their minds. He would have to pick up his horse at Anse Lipscomb's Livery. Lipscomb was a brawler and also he was Hamp Malgren's cousin. A good fight in the early morning would help to relieve the monotony of the rest of the day.

When Doyle entered the stable, moving down the runway, he saw Lipscomb, a wide and tall shadow, standing beside one of the stalls, holding a sheet of yellow paper in his hand. A big man with a heavy frame, Lipscomb was growing a little soft around the middle, but he was still formidable. He had a low forehead and his brows were tufted,

36

forming a solid line across the top of his heavy face.

Doyle moved cautiously. It was cool in the building with its odors of hay and leather and horses. He sniffed the air, reflecting that a man didn't appreciate these small items until he had been cooped up in a jail.

When Doyle tried to make his way toward the far end of the runway, Lipscomb blocked him. He shoved out the piece of yellow paper. 'Six months' feed and stalling for the buckskin,' Lipscomb said, and turned to wink at the townsmen who had clustered in the wide doorway.

Doyle shrugged. He wore the suit he had been arrested in, the suit he might have been married in. But now it was wrinkled, the pants brown and shiny across the seat.

He said, 'Fair enough, Lipscomb. You can deduct it from the rental fees.' Crumpling the paper, Doyle tossed it on a pile of fresh horse droppings in the center of the runway.

Lipscomb balled his heavy fists. He was six inches taller than Doyle, which made him the biggest man in Regency. Loren Pellman had once remarked that Lipscomb might be picked up by a circus sideshow as a freak one day, but they'd never display his brain in a bottle of alcohol after he was dead, because it would be too small to be seen without a microscope.

'Without a gun,' Lipscomb said, peering

37

down at Doyle, 'you ain't tough at all. Now pay up or don't touch that buckskin.'

Doyle turned to a stall. After six months, the buckskin should have been sleek and fat and full of hell. But Doyle could count ribs, and the flanks bore spur marks that had never been there before. A slow anger touched him as he moved into the narrow stall and rubbed the buckskin's muzzle.

He selected a saddle from a peg on the wall, but dropped it when he felt Lipscomb's heavy hand on his shoulder.

Turning at the pressure, Doyle said, 'Well?'

In his wrinkled suit, Doyle didn't look much like the slim rider who had come to Regency last year, his face brown and smooth shaven, wearing good clothes. And Lipscomb said loudly, scornfully, for the benefit of the crowd, 'You ain't putting a saddle on that horse.'

Almost gently Doyle removed the liveryman's hand from his shoulder. 'You claim I owe rental fees?'

'Sure you do.'

'You've been renting the buckskin to every two-bit saddle bum and drummer that hit town, Lipscomb.'

The heavy face took on a puzzled expression. 'Where'd you hear that?' Lipscomb blustered.

'You forget that I could see practically

everything that went on in this town from my cell window,' Doyle said. 'I saw what you did to my horse. And I don't like it worth a damn.'

Lipscomb's bushy brows lowered, and he began to push his shirt sleeves far up on thick forearms. 'My cousin's been aching to settle with you,' he said. 'But maybe I'll soften you up for Hamp.'

Regularly Doyle had chinned himself on the crossbar above his cell window and done pushups on the floor. Jail had not softened him. He dodged the stableman's first rush and hit him a solid smash in the face. As the big man reeled, Doyle struck him again behind the ear. Lipscomb pitched head first into the manure pile where Doyle had thrown the feed bill.

Lipscomb rose dazedly, pawing horse droppings from his shaggy hair. He stood for a moment, glaring, then wheeled for a rifle that was pegged above his office door. Quickly Doyle cut in, extended a foot. Lipscomb tripped and fell heavily. Doyle was about to reach for the rifle when he heard Sol Dinker's nasal voice from the doorway.

He saw the fat deputy with the lank Tom Joplin at his side. Both deputies had elbowed their way through the crowd and now stood with drawn guns, obviously enjoying this display of their authority before the townspeople.

Dinker said again, 'Don't pick up that rifle, Doyle.' When Doyle stood rigid, the deputy said to Joplin, 'Sure be a shame if we had to put up with him in our jail for another six months.'

'Next time,' Joplin said, his jaws working on a chew of tobacco, 'I'd do more than spit on his floor.'

Doyle waited, knowing they wouldn't dare shoot him down in front of these onlookers. Somehow, looking at their faces, Doyle sensed that the men knew this had changed from a simple brawl to something much more serious. The presence of the two deputies had quelled their excitement of a few moments before.

Then the back of Doyle's neck went cold. He had shifted so he could watch both ends of the runway, and toward the rear, by the corral, he saw a gray horse that had wandered in. It stood spraddle-legged, its flanks covered with foam and blood. It stood with head down, reins trailing, a horse that had been ridden nearly to death. On the left flank was the Skull Bar brand. Projecting from a saddle scabbard was a rifle, the butt bearing a large HM cut crudely into the stock. The horse had been ridden by someone in a mighty big hurry, and the HM on the rifle stock could stand for Hamp Malgren.

Then Doyle saw him, a big dark man in his middle twenties. A brutishly handsome man standing in the deep shadows of the rear wall.

'Come out in the light, Hamp,' Doyle said quietly, 'and let the boys get a good look at a man who attacks a woman.'

The crowd turned to look at Malgren. He swaggered to the runway. His small mouth was tight at the corners below his flaring nostrils. 'You don't scare me worth a damn, Doyle,' he said, and spat on the straw-littered floor. His eyes, small and yellow-brown, swiveled at his cousin who stood rubbing a swelling on his jaw. 'What's the matter, Anse?' he demanded. 'I figured you'd beat his head off, then I'd finish the job with a gun.'

Anse glared at him. 'Where'd you come from?'

'Sneaked in when you and Doyle started your argument,' Malgren said in his odd, high-pitched voice.

'Then why didn't you give me a hand?' Lipscomb demanded sourly. He squinted at his cousin. 'Come to think of it, how come you got away from Dutchman's Flats? I thought Gunwright was supposed to keep you boys out there—'

'Shut up,' Malgren said, without looking at his cousin. He stood on the balls of his feet, peering down the runway where Dinker and Joplin stood with the guns in their hands. Some unspoken signal seemed to pass between Malgren and the deputies, for in a moment the latter two holstered their

41

weapons and began shoving the crowd away from the doorway and into the street.

'Clear out, boys,' Joplin said, and spat tobacco juice on the dusty road. 'Fun's all over with.'

As the crowd started away from the stable, Doyle thought, They're going to get the crowd away and let Malgren murder me. His gaze slid to the rifle on pegs above the office door and he carefully began to calculate his chances of reaching it before Malgren shot him.

Malgren shifted his attention to Doyle, and said in his juvenile voice. 'What was it you said to me?'

'You heard me,' Doyle said and took a step toward the rifle. His heart was hammering and the back of his shirt was drenched with sweat. 'There's always men like you who get their guts full of whisky and then catch a girl out alone in the hills.'

Malgren laughed, the sound thin and almost boyish. 'Get the rifle, Anse,' he told his cousin. 'Doyle has his eye on it.' Then he drew his gun.

'Shoot me,' Doyle said, seeing that the doorway had been cleared of possible witnesses, 'and you'll hang.'

He knew it was an idle threat, for Malgren laughed again. Then he flexed his stiff left arm. 'Nobody's going to hang me. Hell, Doyle, you're really loco!' He thumbed back the hammer of his revolver. From a corner of his eye, Doyle saw that Lipscomb had unhooked the rifle from its wall pegs and now gripped it in his big hands.

Malgren said, 'Like I say, you're loco. It was me that catched you and Ellie out in the bushes loving—'

From the doorway a voice said, 'Put up that gun, Malgren.'

Sheriff Conodine's lank form slouched along the runway. The sheriff halted in front of Hamp Malgren. 'Gunwright promised he'd keep you at Dutchman's Flats till Doyle got out of town.'

Malgren's face was red and he seemed unable to reach a decision. But finally he holstered his weapon. 'Doyle beat up my cousin,' Malgren said. 'I was just going to give Anse a hand.'

The sheriff spun on his heel to glare at Doyle. 'Without a gun,' he said, 'I should think you'd have sense enough to hold your temper.'

'I'm not in your jail now,' Doyle said thinly. He felt like adding that Conodine's two deputies now peering in the doorway would have stood by and let a murder take place, but he didn't trust his voice. It had been too close. He was shaking.

Conodine seemed as harassed as he had in the jail office. 'I'll give you a final warning before I leave for the county seat.' He took a deep breath as if trying to frame something distasteful. 'Dinker and Joplin are in charge here in Regency. They don't like you worth a damn, and neither do I, for that matter. Just watch your step or next time we'll put a rope around your neck and end this thing for good.'

'Who'll spring the trap?' Doyle asked, cooler now. 'You or Sid Gunwright?'

The sheriff swore under his breath and turned on Malgren. 'Get back to Dutchman's Flats, Hamp. Stay there for the rest of the day or I'll have you locked up.'

Malgren looked surly, but he did not press his luck. He boarded the jaded gray and wheeled out the rear stable door.

Then the sheriff waited while Doyle saddled his buckskin and stepped aboard. Doyle looked down at Lipscomb, smiling a little at the puffiness on the right side of the man's heavy jaw. Then he lifted a hand to the sheriff and rode out.

The striped barber pole in front of McNear's shop drew him. He racked his horse and spent the next hour getting a shave and a haircut and having a session in the tin tub in the lean-to behind the shop. When he emerged, his face felt lighter without the heavy beard, and his skin was scraped raw. He rode slowly out of town, thinking of what eight hundred dollars would do for him in some new country. Which was better, he

44

asked himself, Gunwright's check or another battle for a hopeless cause? He'd had plenty of hopeless causes, more than his share. Four years of them in the war. But instead of turning back to Pellman's to pick up Gunwright's check, he headed for the Temple Hills. Without a gun he was doomed, and his first project was to get his hands on a weapon of some kind.

CHAPTER FIVE

In the 'Boss Wagon' at Dutchman's Flats, Sid Gunwright leisurely shaved with hot water Skip Harlow had brought him. This wagon was luxury and he had laughingly told Sabrina that she would have decent quarters during roundup. She had said it would be too close to the men; she had no intention of allowing one of them to put his ear to the door at night, or maybe find a corner of the window not quite covered by the curtains. So Gunwright had informed her that such a thing was not possible. The heavy plate mirror above the marble washstand had been built for feminine use. In fact, a standing joke in the Regency country was that his father had been the only cowman who maintained a boudoir for his ladies beside a branding fire.

Sabrina hadn't thought it was funny. She

had sat up on the big bed, looking small and defenseless. Her hair was loose about her nude shoulders and she crossed her arms in front of her as if that could keep him from seeing.

'Don't class me with those women who slept with your father in the boss wagon,' she said. 'I'll bet he never took your mother out there.'

It was Gunwright's turn to be angered. 'My mother was a lady,' he told her.

'And what the hell do you think I am?'

'Put your clothes on and maybe I can tell.'

She threw a mirror at him, and he left the house and went along the walk to Pellman's, almost forgetting to stand on the porch a moment so Doyle, in the cell above, could see him.

By the following Friday she was docile again. He said, 'Doyle gets out next week.'

The lovely face did not change expression. It pleased him to find that she showed no feeling for Doyle. He took her by the wrist and started to lead her upstairs. She jerked away from him.

'Last week you said I wasn't a lady,' she said.

'You know I didn't mean it that way.'

In the big quiet house at the end of Primrose Street, she showed him her teeth in a wicked smile. 'I won't go upstairs with you, Sid.'

He studied her, then said, 'Is it because I made you mad, or is it because Doyle gets out of jail?'

He went upstairs alone. In a few moments she followed him. It gave him a certain satisfaction to know she was afraid of him. But that was last Friday.

Now he had two cups of coffee at the cook fire where he had established camp for a beef gather. The constant sound of cows bellowing for water grated on his nerves. It was going to be another hot one, he reflected, as he tilted back his large, well-formed head and peered up at the morning sky. He removed his hat and scrubbed thick fingers through his short-cropped light hair. He was sweating already and the day was still young. Yesterday, over the Rubios, there had been some clouds that held a possibility of rain. But today they were gone.

Replacing his hat, he fingered the ruby stickpin he always wore in the front of his shirt and watched his riders saddle up for the day's work. In his pale gray eyes was a boldness, a sign to the world that what he wanted he would take. A man not yet thirty, but with a maturity and judgment beyond his years, a man with a certainty of purpose.

Although he had given Sheriff Conodine his word that he would pull his riders to Dutchman's Flats until Doyle could get out of town, he had only a handful of men here.

47

The bulk of his crew was at the headquarters ranch, thirty miles to the west.

During the copper boom at Regency he had sold most of his cattle on the ranch his father had willed him. But now, with copper stocks at their lowest point in seven years, he was forced to push his original dream of extending the Skull Bar to the Rubios. And this drought was giving him the excuse he needed.

Stepping away from the chuck wagon, he called to Clyde Fengean. The foreman took his time about yelling orders at a pair of riders. Gunwright frowned at this discourtesy and watched the riders disappear through a curtain of yellow dust kicked up by the milling cattle.

Fengean ambled over on legs incredibly short for so large an upper body. He had thick arms and shoulders and should have been six feet tall. But it was this very shortness of stature, Gunwright knew, that made Fengean the man he was, cool and deadly and angered at the world so that he seemed completely without conscience.

Fengean chewed on the stem of a scarred pipe. 'You sure this plan will work?' he said, starting to fill his pipe from an Indian rubber pouch he removed from the hip pocket of his denim pants.

'It'll work,' Gunwright said, peering off at the Temple Hills, hazy now in the heat waves that rose from the Flats.

He disliked range work and the rough clothes he was sometimes forced to wear. He preferred the tailored suits he kept in his room at the Regency Hotel. One thing above all others he and Sabrina Hale had in common: they both enjoyed the luxury of good clothes. Sabrina would rather miss a meal than give up a new dress.

Thinking of Sabrina crystallized his resolve. When he had the Skull Bar expanded to its proper boundaries, he would leave Fengean in charge. Last week he had shown Sabrina plans for the house he intended to build on Nob Hill in San Francisco. That was the place to show off beauty such as Sabrina's, not this back door to hell where he had been forced to live most of his life.

'I sent O'Shane and some of the boys to fix up Doyle's house,' Gunwright said. 'We'll use it for a line shack.'

Fengean stared up at Gunwright, his black eyes showing no deference to the man who paid his salary. It was almost as if Fengean resented Gunwright's height that some freak of birth had denied him.

'Skull Bar cows in Temple Hills,' Fengean reflected, touching a match to his pipe, 'will get the hill crowd on our necks.'

'By the time they decide to forget their own petty quarrels, we'll have them boxed.' Gunwright felt an impatience at his foreman's questioning glance. 'Besides, I'll have a right

49

to be in the hills. Doyle's Cross L will be legally mine.'

'You think he'll sign that quit claim deed?'

Gunwirght nodded with emphasis. 'It'll be signed by the time I get back to Regency,' he said.

'Don't be too sure about Doyle.'

Gunwright felt unusually edgy this morning. The cows kept bawling for water. The dust swirled and covered his clothing and was abrasive against the skin. And Fengean seemed to be adroitly crossing him at every turn.

'You can water the herd at Riondo Creek,' Gunwright said shortly, refusing to be drawn into any discussion concerning Kermit Doyle.

Fengean shrugged. With his top-heavy body he looked mild and inoffensive, but the .44 at his belt knew otherwise.

'Push these cows to Riondo Creek,' Fengean said, fingering the point of his chopped-off black beard, 'and we'll have the Barlows looking down gunsights at us.'

'That's the general idea,' Gunwright said irritably. 'We've got a toehold in the hill country now, and with the Barlows out of the way we'll bring the rest of the hill bunch to terms quickly enough.'

Fengean rubbed the bowl of his pipe across a whiskery cheek, trying to put a shine to the coarse grain. 'Speaking of the Barlows,' he said. 'I heard some of the new hands we hired talking about Hamp Malgren.'

'Damn it, Clyde, I told you the incident wasn't to be mentioned to the new men!'

Fengean drawled, 'You know how them stories get around.'

Gunwright's face colored. 'We'll tell our version of it. And see that Hamp tells it.' Gunwright felt a slight displeasure at discussing the subject. 'Let the new boys know it was Hamp who found Doyle and the Barlow girl together. Not the other way around. You understand, Clyde? We want no dissension in our ranks.'

Clyde Fengean spat on the ground. 'How long you figure to keep that son around?'

'I've got use for Malgren,' Gunwright said coldly, hoping Fengean would take the hint and end the discussion.

But the foreman wouldn't leave it that way. 'I'd like to put him in a pit with a black she-bear,' Fengean said. 'That'd be one female he couldn't get the best of.'

Gunwright said, 'Don't let your dislike for the man become too apparent. After all, I intend having him settle the problem of a certain Kermit Doyle once and for all.'

Fengean peered up at Gunwright, a slight malice in his black eyes. 'If I was jealous of a man,' he said quietly, 'I'd sure enough do my own killing.'

Gunwright turned slowly, forcing himself to look at the camp where a hand was riding the morning temper out of a pitching roan. With a shaking hand he removed a cigar from his shirt pocket and slipped off the narrow band which he dropped into the dust. Then he bit off the end of the cigar and put the cigar between his white teeth.

Deliberately he turned back to Fengean and stooped, putting his hands on his knees, the cigar clenched in his teeth. 'Kind of awkward for me to get down to your level, Clyde,' he said coolly, 'but you runts always seem to be the ones with the matches.'

Fengean's face went white. But he struck a match and held it until Gunwright had the cigar going, and blue smoke put a barrier between their tense faces.

Then Gunwright stood up and said in the same cool voice, 'You worked for my father and I owe you a certain loyalty. But don't ever talk to me as you did a moment ago. Because if you do, I'll kill you.'

'All right,' Fengean said quietly. 'I'll remember.'

Trying hard to control his temper, Gunwright watched his foreman cross the camp grounds, tilting from side to side on his short legs. Then Gunwright searched for Hamp Malgren, but could not find him. He tried to question Skip Harlow, but the old cook professed he wasn't hearing so well this morning, and Gunwright was in no mood to shout. Out of sorts, he went down to the rope corral that held the remuda. One of the new hands, a tall, red-haired Texan named Pete Tasker, said he had seen Malgren ride off toward Regency shortly before daylight.

'Why'd you let him go?' Gunwright snarled, his anger directed at what he considered to be an incompetent saddle-bum. Tasker had shown up last week with two partners, Charlie Prince and Al Miller. Because the trio looked grim and were heavily armed, Fengean had hired them for the battle that was to come.

Gunwright said, 'Every man had orders to stay in camp!' Gunwright flung his cigar to the ground and began to curse, finding a certain release in this act.

But Pete Tasker's lips whitened. 'I don't take to that kind of cussing, Mr. Gunwright.'

Something in the man's tone caused Gunwright to halt his tirade. Not that he was afraid, he told himself, but a fight with one of the hands would serve no purpose now. He finally forced a smile. 'Sorry, Tasker,' he said. 'I'm off my feed this morning.'

Shortly before noon Sheriff Conodine rode up, on his way back to the county seat. There was a lack of cordiality in the sheriff's manner. He seemed glum and out of sorts, but ate a noon meal with Gunwright in the boss wagon. Seated at a teakwood table, covered with Chinese carvings, the sheriff commented that this was sure a fancy outfit

53

for a cow camp. And when Gunwright only shrugged it off, the sheriff recounted the near showdown between Malgren and Doyle.

'And Doyle wasn't wearing a gun,' Conodine said, giving Gunwright a sharp look across the oriental table. 'It would have been murder.'

'I'll have a talk with Malgren,' Gunwright promised. Having regained his joviality, since his scene with Fengean and the Texan, Gunwright relayed a joke he had heard last week from a drummer. The sheriff finally lost his moodiness and laughed.

Gunwright walked with Conodine to the latter's horse. 'I expect a little trouble when I move into the hills,' Gunwright said, watching him closely. 'Of course, I have a legal right to be there now that I have Doyle's place, but the Barlows have threatened to slow elk my beef.'

The sheriff digested the statement and shucked the wrapper from a cigar that Gunwright had given him.

'It might be hard to hold some of my boys if they were to catch a running iron on one of the Barlows,' Gunwright said.

Conodine waved the cigar for emphasis. 'I won't hold with lynching a man,' he warned.

And Gunwright instantly countered, 'I'll fire the man who takes the law into his own hands.'

The sheriff seemed satisfied. He boarded

his horse. But in the saddle he said, 'Doyle hadn't signed that quit claim deed when I left town.'

Gunwright gave the sheriff an affable smile. 'He will,' he promised softly. Then, to show Conodine he was fooling with no political amateur, he said, 'I hear the governor may visit over your way next week. Give him my regards.'

The sheriff's mouth opened. 'Never knew you and him was friends.'

'Yes. He was my father's friend,' Gunwright said. He made a mark a little higher than his knee with the flat of his hand. 'I've known Matt since I was that high.'

'So you know him,' the sheriff murmured, mentally building political fences.

'You never know about friends in this country,' Gunwright said pleasantly. 'It's always good to be on the right side.'

An hour after the sheriff had departed, Hamp Malgren rode in on a bloodied horse, half-drunk and mean. Gunwright called him aside, having it on the tip of his tongue to lay the man out for ruining a good horse. But he held his temper. 'You disobeyed my orders,' he said.

They stood on the shady side of the boss wagon. Malgren began to curse. 'I'd have had Doyle, but that damn sheriff butted in.'

Guwnright nodded in sympathy. 'That kind of a play would have cheated you out of

55

eight hundred dollars,' the rancher said.

Malgren's yellow-brown eyes widened with interest. 'Eight hundred dollars? How so?'

'Doyle will be carrying that amount on him when he leaves Regency,' Gunwright said. 'Take some of the new men—those three Texans. Trail Doyle away from town and get him. Give the other boys a hundred apiece. You keep the rest.'

Malgren grinned, fingering a wicked red scar that slanted across his forehead. 'That adds up to a case of whisky,' he said in his high-pitched voice, 'and a week at Mom Lanfield's place.'

'Women and whisky will be the death of you, Hamp,' Gunwright observed.

'Yeah, but what a way to die.' Malgren hurried off through the dust, yelling the names of the three men who were to accompany him.

There was something about Malgren that made a man's skin crawl, Gunwright thought as he chewed on his cigar. But he was thinking of Malgren as possible bait to draw the Barlows out of their hole when the time came. Jeb Barlow and his two sons probably would rush blindly into a trap if Malgren were the bait. It was an interesting potential. With Doyle and the Barlows out of the way, the rest of the hill ranchers, Smalling, Harper, Dunkle and Brome, would come to terms.

Gunwright smiled. Tomorrow he would ride to town. He wondered how Sabrina would take the news of Doyle's passing. She'd better not show any tears, he vowed grimly.

CHAPTER SIX

Kermit Doyle was sheltered in a deep fold of the hills, sweating, while he awaited the approach of the wagon and horsemen he had spotted through the dust some minutes ago. There was a possibility that he would die here in this lonely canyon for there was no gauging the temper of the Barlows.

Hearing the clank of the wagon, the monotonous clop-clop-clop of the team and the sounds of the two horsemen, Doyle sat his horse at the edge of the road. On the wagon seat he could see Jeb Barlow and his red-haired daughter. At sight of him, Jeb pulled up the team while his two sons, Curt and Dave, swung in at the tailgate to glare at Doyle. Dressed in a red-and-white checked shirt and Levis, Ellie sat stiffly beside her father. And she seemed to be holding her breath. Not even her breasts stirred, and there was no other movement at all in her fine young body.

'I heard you were heading for town today,'

Doyle said to Jeb.

Jeb spat over the rim of the off wheel. 'See they let you out,' he said laconically.

Now Ellie turned to look at him, and Doyle could see the play of morning sunlight in her red-gold hair. Her eyes were blue like his own, but of a deeper hue.

Jeb Barlow seemed unable to regain the offensive at seeing their sworn enemy placidly sitting a saddle beside the road, hands folded in plain sight in the saddle horn.

Jeb's stern, uncompromising face was tilted up at Doyle. 'You must want a hole in the brisket, settin' up to us Barlows this way.'

Doyle turned from Ellie's eyes. Curt and Dave were larger than their father, big rangy men who showed no sign of friendliness for the rider on the buckskin.

'If you're heading for town,' Doyle said, 'I'd advise against it. Gunwright's ready to move on us.'

Jeb's mouth firmed so that his lips seemed to disappear into his face. 'When we want your advice,' he said, 'we'll sure as hell get up early to ask for it.'

Curt, young and dark and reckless said, 'I hear Gunwright's pulled his boys to Dutchman's Flats. Ain't no reason for us not to go to Regency.'

'Malgren was in town.'

The three men stiffened. 'That's maybe one of the reasons we're going in,' Jeb said angrily. 'We're tired waiting to catch that son alone in the hills.'

'And besides,' Ellie said, 'I want to get myself some yard goods in Regency. That's my reason for going to town, Mr. Doyle.'

The taciturn Dave said with a short laugh, 'She figures to make herself as purty as Sabrina Hale.'

'Dave—' Ellie's face reddened.

Doyle felt a deep pity for the girl. But the men were dangerous, openly flaunting their views. On the birthday of Jefferson Davis they raised a Confederate flag on a high pole at the side of their 'dobe house where it could be seen for miles, and dared anyone to shoot it down. The flag was the Barlow symbol of defiance in a hostile country that had been largely Union during the War.

Doyle smarted under their steady gaze. Long ago he had ceased to expect any appreciation for what he had done.

'I'm asking no favors,' Doyle said, 'but—'

'Then expect none,' Jeb cut in.

Dave and Curt watched him. Dave was heavy in the neck and shoulders and wore a sweeping mustache too big for his rather narrow face. Curt, two years younger, was shorter than Dave, but Doyle had decided long ago that he was the more dangerous of the two.

'I don't want any thanks for what I did,' Doyle said thinly, trying to get his point across again. From a corner of his eye he saw that Ellie's face had paled at the brutal memory Doyle's words dredged up. 'But I expect a payment,' Doyle finished.

Curt made a sudden movement toward the revolver at his belt, but Jeb saw him and yelled for his youngest son to keep his temper. Reluctantly Curt dropped his hand from the butt of his gun, but he scowled and his eyes were hot as they watched Doyle.

Jeb leaned over in the seat, a thin, irascible old man with gray hair sticking out from under his ancient hat. 'What kind of payment was you talkin' about?' Jeb demanded.

'I need a gun,' Doyle said. 'They ruined mine at the jail. And they won't sell me one in town.'

Jeb rubbed his chin thoughtfully. 'So Gunwright is givin' orders to the sheriff,' he observed dryly. He chuckled then unexpectedly began to curse. 'Yankees!' he snarled, and his face was ugly. 'Gunwright had an uncle with Sherman. I know that for a fact!'

Doyle found Ellie's blue eyes on his face, and for a moment he thought the girl would say something that might ease the tension. But she looked away and he thought, She's beautiful in a wild sort of way. With a nervous hand she fiddled with a button on her shirt that was tight against the pressure of her breasts. She was slim-waisted and the denim

60

pants she wore were snug against hip and thigh.

Jeb Barlow had been watching him intently, and now his lips curled. 'Where was you in the war, Doyle?' he demanded suddenly. 'Or did you have nine hundred dollars to buy yourself out of the Yankee draft?'

Doyle regarded the old man a moment, weighing his reply. Then a stubbornness made him say, 'I came here to forget the war. It's over and done. We've got a new war here. Unless you want to move out and let the Skull Bar have your water.'

Jeb Barlow said, 'Give him your gun, Dave.'

Dave grumbled, but Jeb insisted and finally the older Barlow brother handed over his revolver, butt foremost. After checking the loads, Doyle shoved it into his holster and nodded his thanks.

Jeb Barlow said, 'Riondo Creek is still the boundary. Stay on your own side of it.'

Before Jeb could drive on, Doyle asked a question. 'What kind of shape is my place in?'

Curt gave a short laugh. 'Skull Bar's using it for a line shack.'

The wagon and the two riders moved down the road, and just before they were screened by dust, Ellie looked back. He lifted a hand to acknowledge that spare gesture. But Ellie faced front again and Doyle turned his horse toward Rifle Pass, a slot in the granite cliffs of the Rubios to the north.

In the next three miles the road climbed sharply, and he could smell the clean odor of pines from the high mountains. He pushed the buckskin across Riondo Creek, surprised that it contained only half as much water as he remembered. The creek brawled along the center of a wide canyon before disappearing into the basin sands.

Because he was already on his Cross L range, he moved cautiously, riding with his hand near the butt of the gun Dave Barlow had reluctantly turned over to him. Then, through the aspens ahead he glimpsed the house, and reined in. Seeing it for the first time in months he realized what a sorry place it really was, unpainted, batt-and-board walls, a weed-grown yard trampled by hoofs and the hard heels of riders.

A thin trail of smoke rose from a tin chimney that had been anchored to the roof with guy wires. In the corral behind the house he could see two horses. From somewhere in the distance he could hear the ring of ax blades on timber.

Gun in hand he rose up and dismounted. Leaving his horse in the trees, he crossed the yard. A fat man, his shirt dark with sweat, came out of the house wiping his hands on a grease-stained apron. 'You fellows are back early,' he said. Then, when he rounded a corner of the house and saw Doyle standing alone, his reddish brows shot upward. 'Who the hell are you?' he demanded.

'I was about to ask you the same thing,' Doyle said, and peered over the fat man's shoulder into the house.

The possibility that he might be faced with a crisis here seemed to touch the fat man. He nervously twisted his flour stained hands in the apron. He said hopefully, 'Maybe you're one of the new boys. I hear Gunwright done some hiring yesterday.'

Doyle gave the man a thin smile. 'The name is Kermit Doyle.'

The fat cook's mouth opened. He made a half-hearted effort to reach a gun under the flour-sack apron, but Doyle drew his own weapon and cocked it. He reached over and jerked free the fat man's gun.

'Anybody else around?' he demanded.

The cook seemed to have lost the power of speech. All he could do was shake his head from side to side. He had thinning black hair and laugh wrinkles around his gray eyes. But he wasn't laughing now.

'Rest of the boys are off cutting poles for the new corral,' the cook finally managed to say. He was perspiring and the way he kept looking at the gun Doyle held indicated that he considered it highly probable that he would be shot down in his tracks.

63

Doyle stuck the fat man's gun into his belt, then said, 'Let's talk.'

The man swallowed and said his name was Tim O'Shane. He had been sent up here with four other Skull Bar riders. In the distance Doyle could hear the ring of axes as the crew worked at cutting poles. A crooked grin touched his mouth. The Skull Bar hands would be in a sour mood when they rode in from the cutting grounds. No cowhand, Doyle knew, liked any job that couldn't be done from the back of a horse.

Ordering O'Shane to walk in front of him, Doyle carefully studied the interior of the house through a side window. Satisfied that no one else was about, Doyle herded O'Shane inside. He stood in the center of what had once been his kitchen-parlor. The floor was littered with gear—coiled saddle ropes, saddles, blankets. Against the south wall they had started to build a row of bunks.

Doyle looked at O'Shane severely, angered that Skull Bar would come out here and tear his place apart. 'I suppose you know you're trespassing,' he said.

O'Shane looked scared again. 'I heard you sold out to Gunwright,' he wheezed.

'You heard wrong.' Doyle studied the man. Tim O'Shane had the mark of a drifter on him, a man probably harmless enough in ordinary circumstances. 'I'd hate to shoot another Irishman, O'Shane,' he said, 'so you play my game and you won't get hurt.'

Relief flooded across the fat face. 'I surely will play your game, Doyle,' he promised fervently. 'I surely will.'

When Doyle looked around for his gear and mentioned that it was missing, O'Shane said it had been moved into the shed behind the house. He prodded O'Shane to the shed and they stood together in the small, dusty building. Nostalgia was heavy in Doyle as he saw Sabrina's trunk, still roped as it was the night they had planned to run off to Denver and get married; the night they arrested him for the shooting of Hamp Malgren. Beside the trunk was his own portmanteau and he knew it probably still contained his best suit, the one a New Orleans tailor had made for him. It was odd, he thought, how life had a habit of wrecking a man's plans. Had it not been for riding through Temple Hills that day and finding Hamp Malgren, he and Sabrina would now be married.

He put a padlock on the door and locked it, then took O'Shane back into the house. 'You Skull Bar men are moving today,' he said.

Tim O'Shane licked his lips. 'I'll go right now if you want, Doyle.'

'No, I want you here. The whole crew is getting out.'

'But you can't buck them four fellas,' O'Shane said fearfully, as if already visualizing his own possible ineffectual role in a gun fight.

'We'll see,' Doyle said, Then he jerked his head at the rusted stove where a pot was simmering. 'You go ahead and fix their meal just as if nothing had happened.' Doyle touched the butt of the revolver he had holstered. 'And don't get any ideas about letting them know I'm in here.'

Tim O'Shane gave an emphatic shake of his head. 'I don't want no part of trouble. All I want is a little money to spend and grub and a place to roll my blankets.'

O'Shane worked at the stove, occasionally casting an apprehensive glance at the big man who sat in a shadowed corner in the tipped-back chair.

'How'd you get mixed up in a deal like this?' Doyle asked while O'Shane kneaded biscuit dough.

O'Shane shrugged fat shoulders. 'I was working at the Copperjack. When they started the layoff, I had to find me a job. I didn't have much luck. I missed a lot of meals and was about at the short end of the rope when Gunwright hired me. I used to wrangle horses before I got fat.' He swore under his breath. 'But Gunwright sets me to cooking. A hell of a job.'

'If you've got any brains, O'Shane,' Doyle said, feeling a compassion for this fat man, 'you'll get out. You might get buried up here if you don't.'

It was just at twilight that Doyle heard the sound of horses in the road. He gave O'Shane a final warning. 'Act natural, and you'll be all right.' He paused, looking and the cook's white face. 'You said there was four of them?'

'Four of them rode out of here this morning,' O'Shane whispered, and looked out the door where the first of the Skull Bar men was crossing the yard.

Quickly Doyle stepped into the bedroom and closed the door a crack so he could peer into the combination kitchen and parlor. He drew his gun and waited, feeling a tautness in his chest. A lank man with straw-colored hair crossed to the stove and lifted a pot lid.

'Beans again,' he said disgustedly.

O'Shane was sweating. 'I told Gunwright I wasn't no cook,' the fat man protested. 'Now set down, Lew, and I'll ladle you up some chow.'

Lew Gorling planked his lean frame into a chair and gave O'Shane a critical stare. 'The way you look you'd think you was out cuttin' poles all day. We got the hard work and all you do is stay in the shade and mess with cooking.' Gorling inclined his head to peer closer at O'Shane. 'What's eatin' you, anyhow?'

'Nothing wrong with me,' O'Shane said, but his voice was shaking. He ladled beans onto five plates.

'You oughta be glad you wasn't out cuttin'

down them damn trees,' Gorling continued to grumble. 'A man's used to saddlework, but he ain't used to swinging a goddam ax all day—' Gorling drew back as O'Shane nearly spilled a bowl of beans in his lap. 'Watch what you're doing! You drunk or something?'

'I—I'm all right.'

'If you're all right now,' Gorling said from a corner of his mouth, 'I'd hate to see you when you wasn't.' He thought that was funny, and threw back his head and laughed.

From the crack in the door, Doyle studied the man. Gorling was a typical rider, hard-bitten, grumbling at the chores set for him to do by a tyrant foreman. He wore a big ivory-butted gun. He had already started to eat, not waiting for the others Doyle could hear moving about in the yard. He hoped none of them would stumble on his horse, but considered it unlikely because it was hidden some distance away.

The only one of the bunch he remembered from the old days was Lew Gorling. The other three men who trooped in tiredly, grumbling about the hard work, had been hired since Doyle had spent the winter in jail. The men broke some of the biscuits up into the bowl of beans. In the center of the table was a jug of larrup. This sticky molasses they smeared on with knives.

Tim O'Shane, having seen to the needs of he crew, was about to sit down at his own

68

place. Gorling said, waving a hair-backed hand, 'Put on another plate. Slim will be in in a minute.'

O'Shane froze, his frantic eyes on the bedroom door. 'I only figured you four for supper,' he said nervously.

'Don't worry,' Gorling said. 'You got enough of them damn beans to feed half the Mexican army.' He helped himself to another biscuit. 'Gunwright sent Slim over to tell us to keep an eye out for Kermit Doyle. You seen him around, maybe?'

O'Shane kept wiping his hands on his apron. Perspiration dripped down off his face. It was very quiet in the house, and the four men had paused in their eating to peer up at the fat cook.

Gorling said, 'By God, there is something the matter here.'

O'Shane backed up. 'No. No there ain't. I ain't never laid eyes on Doyle in my whole life.'

Doyle had been debating his next move in the bedroom, hoping he could forestall any move on the part of the Skull Bar men until the fifth rider got in the house. But the unexpected arrival of Slim Dorn had ruined his plan. Even at best it was hazardous trying to get the jump on four men. A fifth only made it more precarious. But now with Dorn in the yard still the odds became too great.

As Doyle backed up from the bedroom

door, he heard Lew Gorling say, 'What the hell's the matter, O'Shane?'

At the bedroom window Doyle peered cautiously out into the yard and saw Slim Dorn. The short, bowlegged man was an old Skull Bar rider, and Doyle had always considered him a friendly sort. But now the chips were down and Dorn was looking straight at the bedroom window from the corral where he had just turned his horse.

'Doyle's in the house!' Dorn yelled. Then something orange bright winked at Doyle and the top half of the window came crashing down, spraying him with glass. In the room behind him he heard chairs kicked back, the rattle of kitchenware against the floor, the crashing of the overturned table as the Skull Bar men got at their guns.

The bedroom door was flung open, and Doyle whirled, throwing a wild shot that made the yellow-haired Lew Gorling jump aside with a curse. Then, without considering the risk, Doyle plunged through the window, striking the ground heavily on his left shoulder. For a moment the fall stunned him; then he began to crawl away where the twilight shadows had thickened near the shed.

From the cover of an aspen, Slim Dorn put two bullets into the house wall. But Doyle was on his feet and running, trying to put the shed between himself and the house. The fact that Doyle seemed in flight, caused Dorn to step boldly away from the sheltering aspen. Doyle saw him as he suddenly veered away from the house. He shot the Skull Bar rider in the upper body. He saw the man pitch forward, try to grasp the trunk of the aspen for support, and then crumple.

Behind him the Skull bar men were crashing across the porch, hoping to pin him outside. Doyle skirted the corral where the horses were milling, threatening to knock down the flimsy barricade in their panic at the firing. He could hear the Skull Bar men coming at a run, firing, and the wicked sound of lead was all about him. Knowing he could never reach the buckskin he had hidden in the aspen grove, without a chance shot bringing him down, Doyle veered toward the corral gate in the thickening darkness. With one hand he flipped up the braided loop of baling wire that held it closed. The gate was flung outward as the panicked horses surged against it. The edge of the gate struck Doyle in the back. The impact sent him sprawling, but he managed to retain a grip on his gun.

He sprang to his feet, expecting to see the Skull Bar men ready to close in. But the horses were thundering across the yard, their hoof beats rocking the ground. He saw Gorling and the men with him dive for safety to keep from being trampled.

Just as Doyle was ready to turn for his

buckskin, he saw Slim Dorn get up off the ground. Dorn, wounded, had crawled toward the house. As Doyle watched helplessly, he saw the bowlegged rider running crookedly, a hand at his stomach. A thick nausea was in Doyle as the wounded man flung up a hand as if to ward off the frantic charge of the horses that were bearing down on him. Dorn screamed once, and then the horses were on him and over him, and he did not move.

Doyle got his horse and rode out. He was perspiring and he felt a vast sickness engulf him. In a way, he blamed himself for Slim Dorn's death, because he had set the horses loose.

From a ridge he looked down, saw Lew Gorling in the light of a lantern one of the men held, looking down at Dorn's body. Gorling took a tarp somebody handed him and dropped it over the body. Then the men went into the house to salvage what they could of the supper.

It's started, Doyle reflected bitterly, as he turned his horse south. He had lost his first battle with Skull Bar at the price of a life, Slim Dorn's. Once he had shot a game of pool with Slim and last summer he had helped the rider pull a calf out of a bog. It was the war all over again. He remembered a brother officer in one of those hopeless and furious cavalry charges, splitting a skull with a saber, the skull of a man in a blue uniform. Later, the officer had come to the tent, his eyes glassy. 'I killed Mike out there today. Mike married my sister and took her north last year.' He had stared down at his saber. And later that night the officer had wedged the hilt of the saber between two rocks and flung himself upon the blade.

Doyle felt raw and bitter inside as he turned his horse down the Regency road. Yes, it was the war again.

CHAPTER SEVEN

Sabrina Hale spent a restless night, and for the second time in as many days she rose early. She crept down the wide carpeted stairway of the twenty-room house, aware of the silence and the emptiness. Only the sound of her slippered feet on the staircase. She wished now, as she had many times in the past, that her Mexican maid, Lita, lived on the premises. At one time she had, but the coming of Kermit Doyle to Regency and subsequently the more reckless life Gunwright insisted she lead when Doyle was jailed, made it impractical to have a maid who might talk in the cantina. So far, the citizens of Regency could only speculate on her life here in this house. They had no proof.

In the kitchen she built a small fire in the

73

stove, and threw fresh grounds into the big pot that was kept on the back of the stove. Just like a cow camp, she thought bitterly. Add grounds to the pot each day until the seventh, when it was strong enough to burn a hole through good boot leather, the cowhands said. Once there had been seven servants living here and Sabrina had never gone downstairs for breakfast until she was fourteen. She'd breakfasted on a big tray in her bed.

As she waited for the coffee to heat, she tried to analyze the nameless fear that seemed to grip her. It wasn't fear of losing her looks. Not yet. Yesterday one of Gunwright's new riders had tipped his hat and looked pleased when she gave him a faint smile. In the hardware she had casually asked the man's name, for he had just purchased some shells. Johnson said he was a Texan and his name was Pete Tasker.

No, the fear was deep and black in some remote niche of her mind. A fear of poverty, she supposed it was. Four months ago an engineer had come out from the east and inspected Copperjack. His report was pessimistic. The meager income she still received would gradually dwindle even further, the engineer predicted.

In a way she felt embittered that fate had touched her with so cold a hand, and so often. She remembered her father staggering home, blind drunk, the day the Copperjack stock broke. A pall had hung over the town that day and the wealthier citizens had repaired to the big room behind Pellman's, there to speak of the tragedy in hushed tones. There were three suicides that first day. And her father might as well have put a gun muzzle in his mouth. The doctor had forbidden liquor in any form, yet later, Sabrina had learned from Pellman, her father had consumed a quart of brandy.

Her father died that first night of the break at Copperjack.

Even as little worked as the mine was now, the stocks her father had owned gave her a fair income. It allowed her to visit San Francisco and Denver once a year. After these journeys she returned with trunks full of clothes. The way she was able to dress made her the envy of every woman in town, and she knew that most of them probably hated her.

She thought of the gay, mad days of Regency, riding with Sid Gunwright in the fancy red-wheeled buggy his father had bought him. Watching Sid, when he was sixteen, throw a handful of goldpieces at some miners' children and watching the youngsters fight and snarl as they scrabbled for the money. On her seventeenth birthday her father had given her a party in the family room at Pellman's. And he brought a chef all the way from a famous hotel in Chicago to supervise the banquet.

That night Burke Gunwright got drunk—she still could remember how the old man smelled of manure through his expensive clothing. Sid's father said that Sabrina should become a Gunwright. And her own father, equally drunk, agreed.

And because in the light of the vague moral code of Regency, they were practically betrothed, the fathers let son and daughter ride home together.

Sid took Sabrina out the back door and they got in the buggy and skirted the main part of town. In the poplar grove behind the big house he pulled her to the ground. Even then she was afraid of him. He was big and arrogant and very sure of himself where women were concerned.

She remembered she had sobbed, not in indignation but in the knowledge that never could she be free of this man.

'I wanted to make sure of you,' Sid had said, smiling down at her in the darkness in his superior way. 'Now you'll have to marry me.'

But she didn't. She kept away from him and she heard the talk that Mom Lanfield, a pleasant, apple-cheeked old lady with dyed red hair, had imported a special girl for Sid Gunwright. The girl was kept locked in a room and only opened the door to Sid.

Sabrina had seen her once, a pale, fragile thing, and she felt disgust.

But Gunwright was persistent, and the older he grew the more vile he became. Then Kermit Doyle had arrived in Regency, and she saw in the tall, brown-haired man a chance to escape this town. But he had been found one day with a cheap hill girl, and had been arrested. He was no better than Sid Gunwright who had his own brand of hill girl at Mom Lanfield's. But Gunwright had money, and after Doyle was locked up in the Regency jail, he explained the plans for expanding Skull Bar, and the eventual turning over of the ranch to Clyde Fengean's management. Then a house on Nob Hill in San Francisco.

Sabrina made her choice the second night of Kermit Doyle's imprisonment.

'I'll be coming to town every Friday night,' Gunwright said.

Only for a moment did she close her eyes. Then she opened them and smiled. 'I'll be here,' she said, 'waiting.'

He kissed her then, and she drew back, her hazel eyes narrowing. 'One thing I won't be. Second to a girl at Mom Lanfield's.'

At first Sid had denied that any such agreement with Mom Lanfield existed. But when she convinced him she was aware of this, he finally agreed to send the girl on her way. Next day Sabrina had seen her in front of the Regency House, sitting on a portmanteau, looking forlorn as she waited for the stage. For a moment Sabrina was tempted to give her some money, but to go up to such a woman in broad daylight, much less speak to her, would cause much gossip. Already there had been too much talk concerning her activities.

Sabrina finished her coffee and then Lita came. Lita started cleaning up the house, singing a Mexican song under her breath.

'Dust the furniture in the parlor,' Sabrina told the girl.

Lita looked perplexed. 'But this is not Friday . . .'

Sabrina felt the blood drain from her face. Briefly she toyed with the idea of firing the girl. But that would solve nothing. She wanted to laugh. She had been so careful to keep these clandestine meetings with Sid a secret.

'What's so special about Friday night, Lita?' she asked, seeking to draw the girl out.

Lita shrugged a fat brown shoulder. 'I do not know. But on Saturday I always find the butts of *cigarros*.'

She frowned. She would have to caution Sid about leaving his cigars around.

*   *   *

After a night in the hills, Doyle rode to

Regency, pondering his problem. Without some backing from the hill crowd he stood little chance of throwing the Skull Bar off his Cross L, and right now that seemed completely hopeless. When he pulled into town in midmorning, he caught sight of Sabrina's yellow house through the poplars, and a bitter thought caused him to turn his horse that way.

Seeing no horses in the yard, he left the buckskin in the grove and crossed to the rear door which he found unlatched. From the front part of the house came Sabrina's voice, giving orders to her Mexican maid, Lita. He stood in the big kitchen, nostalgia working in him for a moment. From a cooler beside the sink pump he took a bottle of beer and a chunk of yellow cheese.

Leaning against a meat block, he stared around the big kitchen. It represented wealth.

He waited until Sabrina came to the kitchen, her face showing her vexation at some household problem. At sight of him, she turned white and looked back into the parlor. Then she carefully closed the kitchen door.

'You shouldn't be here,' she said tensely. 'Not in broad daylight.'

'I couldn't wait,' he said. As he finished his beer, he noted the same old dissatisfaction in her eyes. He wondered at the cause.

She said with growing irritation, 'You're

taking a lot for granted. I thought when I didn't visit you at the jail you'd know how I felt.'

He laid aside the empty beer bottle and dusted his hands of the cheese crumbs. 'Just thought I'd come by and tell you that I saw your trunk.' He watched the lovely, intent face. 'It's still at the Cross L.'

'Did you destroy it?' she asked breathlessly.

'No. I didn't have a chance.'

'But you will,' she said hopefully, and added, 'Wait here, Kermit.' She went into the front part of the house. In a few moments, through a side window, he saw Lita, the Mexican woman, walking along the brick path to the street.

Moving to the parlor, he looked around at all the familiar objects. The room was as he had pictured it during those long nights in jail. Heavy draperies at the windows screened the sunlight from the rose-colored carpet. On a cherrywood sideboard, beside a leather couch, he saw an unsmoked cigar, and a faint smile touched his lips. He sank to the couch, thinking that this was his first luxury in six months. He stretched out his legs and felt a vast contentment flow through him.

To have money, he thought, to be without the everyday worries that plague most humans. Then he thought of the wealth this town had once enjoyed. Money had made the citizens soft and when the bubble broke they were not up to facing reality. He had heard about the suicides. And Sabrina's father had died in this house the night the Copperjack was practically closed down. He remembered without humor a story Pellman had told him of a rancher who had sold his property and purchased Copperjack stock. The man became so used to high living that when the crash came, he cried: 'I'm broke. Busted flat. I've only got thirty thousand dollars left.' Then before anyone could stop him he plunged up the outside stairway at Pellman's and hurled himself from the roof.

Sabrina entered the room and he noticed that she had fixed her hair. 'I see you haven't changed things in the parlor,' he said. 'How is it upstairs?'

'You'll never know,' she said stiffly.

But he ignored her. 'You were talking of pink curtains for your bedroom.' Finding a slight amusement in her obvious anger, he added, 'The last time I was up there they were blue.'

Her mouth tightened. 'I want you to understand that we won't continue as we were before—before you were arrested.' She lowered herself gracefully into a fiddleback chair, clasped her hands and leaned forward to peer at him. 'You understand what I'm trying to say, Kermit?'

Doyle laughed, then sobered. 'Just why

you desert me?' She started to speak, but he held up a hand, cutting her off. 'You told me you wanted to run off to be married, because you wanted no ceremony in Regency where your father had died so recently. Loren Pellman drove you out to my place with your trunk. We were to drive to Canton and take the stage to Denver and be married there.'

'There was nothing wrong with that,' she said impatiently. 'Besides, it's all in the past. I don't even want to think about it.'

'I don't either,' he said sharply, and she looked at him. 'You had a good reason for wanting it that way. Not out of any sense of mourning for your fahter, but because of Gunwright. You were afraid of him. I was a fool not to suspect.'

She looked down at her hands clenched in her lap and some of the defiance seemed to go out of her. 'You asked why I deserted you. I'll tell you why.' She looked up at him and her long hazel eyes were narrow at the corners as her mood switched as was so characteristic of her. 'The day before we were to leave for Denver you were found in the hills with Ellie Barlow in your arms!'

He shook his head at her. 'You don't really believe Malgren's side of it.'

'You tried to kill him,' she said, showing her teeth, 'so he wouldn't be able to spread he story about you and Ellie!' She had rked herself up and her shoulders trembled.

'You're wrong about it,' he said. 'So dead wrong.'

'Then what really happened?' she demanded.

'You could have heard my testimony,' he reminded her, 'if you'd taken the time to attend the trial.' Then he added, 'But as long as you didn't, I'll tell. That day I had been chasing some cows out of the brush when I heard a woman scream. I cut over that way and found them. Ellie's shirt was torn, and one side of Malgren's face was bleeding where she had clawed him. When Malgren drew a gun, I shot him.'

She put a hand to her breast, her gaze intent. 'If your story is true, then you're a fool, Kermit. Malgren wasn't the first Skull Bar man she's been with—'

'That's Malgren's talk,' he said coldly. 'I'd kill him twice if it could be done. But he's through in this country and not even Gunwright can protect him now.'

'Men are disgusting at times,' Sabrina said.

'But you'd be unhappy without them, Sabrina.' He settled back against the soft cushiony support of the leather-backed couch. 'I need you,' he said, and voicing it set his mind to seething.

'I loved you once, Kermit,' she said. 'But not now.'

He gave her a thin smile. 'You're an

opportunist, Sabrina.'

She studied him, noting how different he looked from the time she had seen him on the street, bearded and shaggy-haired and unclean. 'Perhaps I am an opportunist,' she agreed. 'But this country is going to be a bloody battleground. I'm alone in the world, so it's imperative that I be on the winning side.'

His lips curled. 'Don't make me lose my last shred of respect for you.'

He saw the instant hurt in her eyes and he realized he had wounded her vanity. A roaring sound outside caused him to shift his gaze to a break in the curtain that covered the front window. Through the poplar grove he saw the noon stage roar down on Regency, whipping up a great cloud of dust which curled among the trees like yellow smoke.

When the clatter had died, he said, 'It's been six months since I've been even this close to a woman.' He leaned over and placed a hand on her silken knee. She jerked it away, but a flush had touched her cheeks.

'Kermit, you should get out of Regency. I don't love you and Gunwright hates you. And though you belong to the hill crowd, you'll get no sympathy from them because of the Barlows. They despise you for blackening Ellie's name at the trial.'

'Yesterday the Barlows could have killed me,' he said. 'Maybe they would have if it hadn't been for Ellie in the wagon.' He leaned forward again. 'There's one thing you've forgotten. I didn't *ask* Ellie to testify in my defense.'

Sabrina gave a short laugh, and he knew she was disturbed and angered and unable to cope with the situation. The planes of her breasts, held above a corseted basque, were deep with color as was her throat and her face. And he could see a thin bold shine in her eyes that he remembered so well. But she was fighting it desperately.

'The Barlows believe in the purity of their women,' she said, and her voice was unsteady. 'In their eyes you're as much to blame as Hamp Malgren.'

He gave her a sardonic smile. 'You make it sound pretty grim for Kermit Doyle.'

Leaning forward, he caught the sweet scent of her dark hair. He grabbed her wrist and suddenly pulled her roughly across his lap. She tried to struggle, but in a moment gave it up, for his hands held her. She was turned so that her breasts were forced against his arm. For a moment she stayed as she was, then twisted aside.

'So there's no difference between you and Malgren,' she said. 'What you can't have you take by force.'

'It's an idea,' he said, holding her two wrists in the powerful grip of one hand. He increased the pressure and she winced at the pain, but her hazel eyes were glowing and she rested her head against his shoulder. In her struggles her hair had come unpinned and now a lock of it fell softly against the back of his hand. He turned her loose, but she made no effort to get off his lap.

'Damn you, Kermit,' she said without looking at him. 'You're so very strong. I thought jail would soften you.'

He extended a hand to the cherrywood table behind the couch, picked up the unsmoked cigar and held it between his fingers. She watched him curiously for a moment, then color faded from her cheeks when she guessed the trend of his thinking.

'You can't fight Skull Bar,' she said tremulously. 'And even if you could, there's Hamp Malgren.'

'I can handle him.' Doyle slipped a hand up the sleeve of her upper garment and felt her arm warm to his touch.

She stiffened. Then she said, 'I'm so confused, Kermit.' She drew her head back, peering at him through her dark lashes, and there was a sulky air about her. 'I'm going to Denver next month,' she said and her red mouth stirred in a faint smile. 'If you were there at the same time, we could see each other.'

He smiled. 'We could *see* each other?'

Color touched her lovely face. 'Why not?'

'Ever heard of having your cake and eating

it, too?'

He rose suddenly, one hand under her body, and to keep from falling she threw her arms about his neck. He carried her toward the stairway that led to the second floor. At the foot of the stairs he stopped and set her down. He lowered his head suddenly and found her mouth, and felt her lips move frantically under his. She bit him and he tasted blood.

After a moment, she whispered, 'You're so unpredictable. For a moment, I thought you hated me.' She put a hand to her flushed face. 'Where did you leave your horse?'

'In the poplars.'

'Put him out of sight in the carriage house.'

'What about Gunwright?'

Without thinking, she said, 'He'll be at Dutchman's Flats all day.' Then she stiffened as he dropped the cigar he had been holding to the carpet and deliberately ground it with his heel.

'One thing people forgot in this town,' he said coldly. 'I could see a lot from my cell window. Anse Lipscomb forgot it. You forgot it.' He gripped her by the arms. 'I could see your house, Sabrina—at night. At first, I was hurt and mad. But gradually I got over that. I got over it so well that I laughed every time Gunwright stopped in front of Pellman's and lit a cigar. He was so damned childish. He wanted me to see his progress from your house to the saloon. He—'

'Kermit!' she screamed at him, but he turned and walked through the kitchen and out the back door. To hell with the payment he had intended taking from her. He'd only have punished himself worse than Sabrina if he'd collected.

CHAPTER EIGHT

Sid Gunwright held a leisurely pace toward Regency, sparing his horse because of the heat which lay across the Flats. When he rode through the wide doorway at Lipscomb's Livery, the stableman came out of his office to take the horse. Gunwright slipped to the straw-littered runway, noticing that one side of Lipscomb's face was swollen and discolored.

'Have you seen Kermit Doyle around?' Gunwright asked, and smiled inwardly when he saw the bright hatred in Lipscomb's eyes. The big man put a hand to the puffy side of his face as if in memory. 'I forgot,' Gunwright said. 'The sheriff told me you and Doyle had a set-to.'

Lipscomb's small eyes were wicked. 'You ask if I seen Doyle? Yeah, I seen him,' Lipscomb talked with difficulty, probably because of a bruised jaw. 'Yesterday I seen

Doyle talking to Sabrina Hale on the street.'

Gunwright stiffened but with an effort he held himself in. He would show no anger in front of this cousin of Malgren's. After all, Sabrina had given him her word that there had never been anything between her and Doyle.

'Let's not get excited about a chance meeting on the walk,' Gunwright warned, and turned for the door.

'That ain't all,' Lipscomb said in a tight, strained voice, 'I see Doyle sneak in the back door of Sabrina's house—'

Gunwright wheeled, drew an ivory-butted revolver from his belt and jerked back the hammer. Lipscomb braced his big, stupid body against the smash of the bullet.

'Repeat after me, Anse,' Gunwright said in a cold and deadly voice. 'Say this: "I am a damned liar!"'

Lipscombe stood frozen in terror, one hand on his chest as if it could ward off the crashing impact of lead. Then his voice screeched from his big throat. 'I'm a liar, Mr. Gunwright. I am a damned liar!'

Gunwright holstered his weapon. A pulse throbbed at his temple and there seemed to be a red curtain before his eyes, distorting his vision. He looked away so Lipscomb could not see the pure agony of hate on his face. It took him a full minute to control himself to the point where he could speak.

He removed two gold pieces from his pocket and pressed them into Lipscomb's hand. 'Do me a favor, Anse.'

'Sure, Mr. Gunwright.'

'Hunt up your cousin. He'll be somewhere west of town, waiting for Doyle. Tell Hamp to make Doyle's death as unpleasant as possible and then to bring his body to town.'

'Sure, Mr. Gunwright.'

Gunwright clenched his fists, staring toward Sabrina's house that was barely visible through the poplar grove. 'It's good for some people to view a corpse,' he said as if to himself.

Lipscomb jammed the money into the pocket of his overalls and hurried to catch up a horse, his knees so weak he nearly stumbled. Gunwright left the livery and made his way slowly toward the poplar grove.

Sabrina was turning for the stairs when she saw him standing in the doorway that led from the kitchen. Something about his face frightened her. Rarely had she seen him dressed in his rough range clothing, covered with alkali dust, his eyes bloodshot. And he needed a shave.

'I didn't expect you, Sid,' she said in a tight voice. She started for the parlor, thinking he would follow. When he didn't follow her, she looked around to see him still in the kitchen doorway. His eyes were small and ugly and the corners of his mouth were white.

'Is something the matter, Sid?'

'Beer will make you fat, Sabrina.'

She frowned. 'I've never had a bottle of beer in my life,' she said. Then a cold fear touched her, for he now extended the hand he had been holding behind his back. His thick fingers were gripping the neck of an empty beer bottle.

Only for a moment was she stunned; then instinctively she took the offensive. 'Don't stand there with an empty bottle,' she said. 'Throw it in the trash barrel.'

Slowly he came along the hallway and she hoped the color was not leaving her face. He must not see her pale or upset. For she knew his wrath so well. Never had he seemed so formidable, and suddenly she had an unholy horror of the bargain she had made with this man.

His voice flicked at her like a lash: 'Have you seen Kermit Doyle?'

Her mind moved swiftly. 'On the street.' She forced herself to laugh and thought, My God, I sound hysterical. 'I bade Doyle good-by. Don't tell me you're jealous of him!'

He seemed to relax, and his smile was almost genial. For an instant she thought she had convinced him. Then she saw that the white had not left the corners of his mouth, and her breasts seemed to swell so that the constriction of the corseted basque was almost unbearable.

Gunwright said, 'You know why I sent him to jail, don't you?'

She made no reply, only stared at the eyes which filled her with terror. 'What you did to Doyle was your own business, Sid,' she said, and her voice was pinched and frightened.

'I capitalized on Hamp Malgren's fool play with the Barlow girl,' Gunwright went on, still in his easy voice. 'I twisted the story into something that took Doyle away from you for six months.'

A wild pulse throbbed at her temple and she thought bitterly, So it was true about the Barlow girl. Malgren had attacked the girl, and Doyle had interfered.

'It only proves that you're shrewd, Sid,' she said, and went to him. She stood on tiptoe and kissed him on the cheek. She pressed herself against him, sensing in her fear that if he wanted her he would forget all else.

But he suddenly flung her away from him so that she fell against the staircase. It stunned her and the blow loosened the pins in her hair so that it tumbled about her white face. Numbly she watched him smash the beer bottle against the post. He still retained the neck in his hand. He came toward her and gently pressed the shattered end of the bottle against her neck.

'If I thought Doyle had been here this day, I'd tear out your throat.' He spoke mildly as if he might be raising the ante in a stud poker game and did not want to betray with his tone the fact that he had aces back to back. 'I won't stand for another man touching you.'

She began to sob, and she clung to the bannister with bloodless fingers. 'Why is it different?' she cried. 'You had your girl at Mom Lanfield's—'

He lowered the jagged piece of beer bottle glass to the upper slopes of her white breasts and pressed down. She felt pain and bit her lips. Then he removed the weapon. She looked down, seeing the small red marks on her flesh.

'It's different, that's all,' he said, a queer note in his voice. 'And if Doyle—'

From some hidden corner of her mind a shred of hope emerged, and she sensed that scorn might triumph where her own passionate entreaty had failed. She glared at him through her tears.

'You don't have much confidence in yourself,' she cried at him, 'if you think I'd turn to Kermit Doyle!'

For a moment she saw his face was contorted and he lifted his right hand. She thought he would rake the bottle end across her face and she closed her eyes and waited for the pain.

But he lowered his hand. 'Lipscomb claimed he saw Doyle sneak in here.'

'You'd believe that liar?' she said scornfully. He seemed not quite so confident

in his convictions and with that she took
heart. 'I knew you were jealous, Sid, but
this—' She lifted her hands in a gesture of
exasperation.

'Maybe I am jealous,' he agreed. He
dropped the bottle and put an arm about her
waist. He led her into the parlor and then
halted and she saw him staring down at the
cigar that had been crushed against the
carpet. 'Careless of me,' he murmured. 'I left
a cigar on the table. I remember—'

'It must have fallen to the floor and was
stepped on,' she said quickly.

She felt his shrewd appraisal as he said,
'Somebody could have tromped that cigar in
anger. Somebody who doesn't like me.'

'That's ridiculous,' she said. She tried to
step away from him but he held her tightly.

His eyes searched the room carefully. 'I've
put some of my men out at Doyle's place,' he
said.

She froze, a new and greater fear in her.
'Isn't it customary to wait until you have a bill
of sale before you move in?'

He turned on her. 'How do you know
Doyle hasn't sold out to me?' he demanded.

She managed a shrug. 'I don't. I'm only
guessing.'

She wondered if he knew her knees were
trembling. Swiftly she thought of the night
she had planned to run away with Doyle,
driving through Rifle Pass to Canton and

catch the Denver stage.

But something had gone wrong that night. Riders had surrounded the house. When Doyle learned it was because he had shot Hamp Malgren, he had stepped outside and given himself up. And Sabrina had hidden in the house until they were gone. She remembered how desperately she had tried to move her trunk into Doyle's wagon, but it was much too heavy for her. Frightened, she had driven back to Regency.

If Sid Gunwright ever found that trunk filled with her clothes at Doyle's place...

Gunwright said, 'You haven't explained why there was an empty beer bottle in your kitchen.'

She almost laughed with relief when she saw it wasn't the trunk that concerned him. She had thought that perhaps his men, when they moved in at the Cross L, had discovered it. 'Lita had a friend over while she cleaned the kitchen,' Sabrina said easily. 'I suppose he helped himself to a bottle of beer from the cooler.'

'Yes, that could be it,' Gunwright said thoughtfully. Then he added, 'We'll have supper at the hotel tonight.' He dropped his arm from about her waist and started for the door.

'Aren't you staying, Sid?'

'I'll call for you later,' he said with a shake of his head. 'Now I have a little business about a quit claim deed.'

When he had gone and she could hear him moving along the brick walk to the street, the strength suddenly went out of her legs. She sank to the floor. Through the hall doorway she could see the shards of bottle glass on the carpet. Suddenly reaction set in and she began to sob, but there were no tears. A corner of her mind silently screamed the name of Kermit Doyle. He was responsible for this. How she hated him ... hated him ... hated him. She beat her fists against the carpet.

CHAPTER NINE

From the window of Link Johnson's hardware, Doyle saw Sid Gunwright, dressed in a black suit, step out of the Regency Hotel and move along the walk. He was an impressive man, Doyle had to admit, square of shoulder, walking lightly for so large a man. There was something arrogant in the way he wore his hat, and in the angle of the cheroot that projected from his lips. He saw Gunwright enter Pellman's.

Doyle moved out into the heat, noticing a scattering of clouds overhead. It could mean rain, just a slim possibility of one spring storm before the full heat of summer bore down. He felt indecision on him and blamed it partly on the scene with Sabrina. She was unsettling to a man's nerves, and much as he despised her, he felt a faint regret that he had not accepted the promise that had glowed in her eyes.

He took a moment, easing the gun at his belt to a more comfortable position. Then he moved up the street. In front of the New York Store he saw Harvey Brome's family in their wagon: the hill rancher's wife, Agnes, the two young boys, and the older daughter Doris. Last fall, he reflected bitterly, he had danced with the pleasant, brown-eyed Doris.

He crossed the street and removed his hat. But Mrs. Brome had seen him coming. She whispered something to the children and looked away. Doyle felt the snub, and thought bitterly, They believe the story about Ellie and me.

The oldest boy, Jess, grinned despite his mother's warning not to speak to Doyle. 'Howdy, Mr. Doyle,' he said. He was freckled and blue-eyed and resembled his slow-moving father not at all. The younger boy, Alex, was shy.

When it was obvious that Mrs. Brome did not intend to speak, Doyle said, 'How's everything between you and Curt Barlow, Doris?' He remembered that at the dance Curt had given him some black looks when he danced with the girl.

Doris looked up. She wore a sunbonnet and a gingham dress and her eyes were unhappy. 'Momma says Curt and I can't get married.'

Mrs. Brome twisted around in the wagon seat, her eyes small and bright. 'Young uns got no chance in these terrible times, Mr. Doyle!' she cried so loudly that people on the street turned to stare. 'And it's men like you that make this a horrid world!'

'Mrs. Brome—'

She cut him off, her mouth small and bitter. 'I won't have my Doris marryin' with Curt Barlow. Not when Curt may get shot in this war that's comin'.'

Doris had tears in her eyes. 'Momma you forget that you and Poppa married the year the 'Paches cleaned out the Big Bend. Times was terrible then, too—'

'Shut up, Doris!' She slapped Doris across the face, and the girl drew back, sullen and angry. 'And as for you, Mr. Doyle, I should think you'd hang your head in shame! You and that Barlow girl! I always knew them Barlows was short on God's teachings, but I never thought the gal would lay up with a man.'

'Momma!' Doris sat up straight in the seat, her face flaming.

Mrs. Brome turned white with embarrassment, but it did not dim her rage. 'You keep away from my kids, Doyle! I'm warnin' you! I find you lollygaggin' around my Doris and I'll see you whipped and then hanged!'

Doyle put on his hat, his face grim. 'That kind of talk will drive your daughter away from your house, Mrs. Brome.'

He gave Doris a wan smile, but the girl was staring straight ahead, her small figure rigid. Jeff and Alex, the two boys, looked stunned. They sat in the wagon bed inspecting their hands.

Now he knew why Harvey Brome always had that hang-dog air about him. No wonder, with a shrew of a wife like Agnes.

When he entered Pellman's, he saw Harvey Brome, a small and worried man, talking to Sid Gunwright at the bar. As soon as Brome noticed Doyle in the doorway he muttered something to Gunwright and hurriedly left the saloon, eyes downcast.

Gunwright said pleasantly, 'I was afraid you were going to ride off with empty pockets, Doyle.' He jerked his head at Loren Pellman, who stood stiffly behind his bar, a pall of uncertainty on his plump face. The saloonman laid the check and quit claim deed on the bar, then stepped back. His eyes seemed to say, Don't blame me for my part in this, Kermit.

Gunwright said, 'Sign your name to the deed and the check is yours. They'll honor it at the bank. You'll ride out of Regency with

99

eight hundred dollars in your belt.'

Doyle only smiled.

'That kind of money will carry you for quite a ways,' Gunwright reminded him.

A crowd was gathering in the saloon, drawn by that intangible threat of approaching trouble. Townsmen and loafers and drifting riders slipped through the doors to order drinks at either end of the long bar. Pellman and his bartender were busy.

'Human nature,' Doyle observed, not looking at the glass of whisky Gunwright had poured for him from a bottle on the bar. 'They'll risk their necks on the chance of a stray bullet, just to see the blood letting.'

Gunwright's gray eyes showed a faint amusement as he glanced at the gun at Doyle's belt. 'There'll be no blood letting,' the rancher said. 'We understand each other.'

Pellman had placed a bottle of ink and a pen on the bar. Gunwright inclined his head toward them. 'Sign your name, Doyle.'

Doyle made no move to sign.

Gunwright said, 'So you refuse my offer?' There was little outward anger, but the corners of his mouth that held a cigar showed white halfmoons from the inner pressures he seemed anxious to hide.

'Eight hundred dollars isn't much pay for six months in jail,' Doyle said quietly. He picked up the check and the deed, tore them into small pieces and let them drift toward a cuspidor.

There was a shuffling of feet at the bar, and those nearest the two men moved quickly away.

Gunwright said, still with no apparent malice, 'Doyle, I wish you luck.'

Silence was tight in the barroom. A man coughed and the sound was loud as a gunshot.

Doyle said, 'Some of your boys moved in at the Cross L. I don't like it.'

'So?'

'And I'm beginning to wonder what happened to my cows.'

Gunwright touched the ruby stickpin in the front of his shirt, toyed with it a moment as if letting the silence drag on for effect. 'You know how cattle are,' Gunwright said, obviously talking for the benefit of the men who stood with mouths open, those in the rear of the crowd on tiptoes or chairs. 'When there's nobody to look after them, they drift. We'll start spring roundup next week. You're welcome to send a rep or come yourself and cut out your Cross L cows.'

'I'll be there at roundup,' Doyle said.

'Personally I think you're foolish not to take my offer. Malgren has sworn to even his score with you, and there's nothing I can do to prevent that.' Gunwright pushed a cigar along the lip of the bar. 'At least, have one of my cigars.'

Doyle did not pick up the cigar. He said, 'You ought to be more careful where you leave these. A man could back-track you easily from the cigar bands you leave around.'

For a moment Doyle wondered if he had prodded the big man too far, for the rancher's heavy features were no longer bland. Get it over with, he told himself, and waited for Gunwright to make a move.

But Sid Gunwright made a visible effort at self-control. In a moment his features were composed. But there was still something wicked in his eyes.

'Enjoy your beer this morning, Doyle?' he asked softly.

Wariness touched Doyle, for suddenly he recalled the empty beer bottle he had left in Sabrina's kitchen. Despite what she had done to him he had no wish to see her face Gunwright's wrath. Doyle shrugged. 'I never drink beer before noon. Never.'

He turned then and saw Loren Pellman wiping his moist face on a bandanna. Doyle pushed his way through the crowd and went outside.

The Brome wagon had gone, and he moved along the street, a black despair descending on him. He felt utterly helpless, knowing after the scene at Pellman's that Gunwright wasn't going to be goaded into a fight until he had the deck stacked his way. He was too clever to be stampeded. Once again Doyle was tempted to quit this country. That had been his original intention. But he was a stubborn man and Conodine had practically ordered him to take Gunwright's offer. Then he had seen Sabrina again. But worst, Gunwright had been so confident of Doyle moving out that he had sent a crew to make a line shack at the Cross L.

In front of Link Johnson's hardware he noticed the Barlow wagon. Through the window he saw Jeb and his two sons just picking up bulky packages from the counter. Doyle entered, and the three Barlows stood stiff and formidable. He looked around for Ellie, but did not see the girl.

Crossing to the counter, Doyle said, 'We've got a fight on our hands, Jeb. If we don't stick together Gunwright will move in on us.'

The three men measured him. 'Gunwright buy you out?' Jeb asked thinly.

'I just tore up his check down at Pellman's.'

Link Johnson peered over the tops of his square spectacles at Jeb. 'Like I've told you, I got to be neutral in this. But Doyle's a good man, and you'll need all the help you can find. Forget your grudge.'

Curt Barlow said, 'Anybody but Doyle and I'd say yes. But him—' He put a hand to his gun.

Jeb lifted a hand as if to slap his youngest son across the face. It was a ridiculous gesture, for Curt towered above his father. But it had the desired effect. Curt shut his mouth.

A commotion in the street caused them to turn toward the front windows. A horseman moved down Primrose Street, leading another horse that bore a bulky object, wrapped in a blood-smeared tarp lashed to the saddle. The Barlows and Link Johnson stepped quickly to the window to peer outside and speculate on the possibilities of this grim procession. Doyle trailed over, feeling a little sick as he looked down the street and saw that the rider was Lew Gorling. The Skull Bar man was gesturing at Sid Gunwright who had come to the walk in front of Pellman's to stand in the growing crowd. Gunwright said something to the yellow-haired Gorling, and the rider took the horses in the direction of the jail.

Doyle watched the men, Gunwright in the lead, move quickly toward the jail. He said, 'I told you to get in the undertaking business, Link.'

Link Johnson turned, his face a little pale. 'Who was it, Kermit?'

'Slim Dorn. He was at Cross L last night when I rode in.'

Johnson looked at him in amazement. 'You mean you tried to throw out the Skull Bar single-handed?'

'There were five of them at the house,' Doyle said. 'I was going to wait until they all

104

started eating at the table. Then I was going to make my play.' He shrugged. 'But Slim Dorn was in the yard. I hadn't figured on him at my back.'

Jeb Barlow had been peering at Doyle, a grudging admiration in his eyes. 'We're having a meetin' at Canton, Doyle,' he said. 'Day after tomorrow.' He and his two sons stepped to the counter and picked up their heavy packages that were wrapped in newspapers. Jeb went on, 'As long as Gunwright ain't run you out with your tail between your legs, you're welcome to the meeting.'

Doyle said, 'Thanks,' then shifted his attention to the dark and surly Curt. 'Doris Brome was in town a while ago. She wants to get married. Might be you could have a talk with Harvey and convince his wife that—'

A quick interest had brightened in Curt's eyes and for the first time since Doyle had known him, some of the meanness seemed to leave his mouth. Then he said, 'Keep out of my business, Doyle.'

The three Barlows trudged out with their packages.

'Looks like they bought out the store,' Doyle observed.

'Cartridges,' Link Johnson said, shaking his head. 'Ammunition for sixgun and rifle.'

'If they're smart,' Doyle said, 'they'll clear out of town.'

'But they won't. Old Jeb says as long as they're in town he and the boys will sit around on the chance that Hamp Malgren might ride in.'

'The fools,' Doyle said under his breath, but made up his mind also to stay in town. After all, tenuous as it was, the Barlows had cast their lot with him in the simple act of inviting him to the meeting of hill ranchers at Canton.

Link Johnson said, 'If I'd been in your shoes, Kermit, I'd have taken Gunwright's offer.' He sighed. 'But then I ain't you. I just admire your nerve.'

Doyle started for the door as a woman put a hand on the knob. He opened the door for her and tipped his hat.

'Afternoon, Miss Lanfield.'

Mom Lanfield looked at him in some surprise. Her hair was a flaming red, obviously dyed. She wore pearl earrings, and a double row of red beads circled her neck. Flamboyant as she might look, Doyle could not help but remember hearing that on the day of the Copperjack decline—when the bank, also long since bankrupt, had foreclosed ruthlessly—Mom Lanfield had rented the top floor of the Regency House so families caught in the panic could have a roof over their heads before they got out of town. And the dining room was free to those who could not afford to pay. And they said she

106

spent over two thousand more in buying stage tickets for those who could not afford to leave.

The town, in appreciation, had erected a small stone plaque in her honor, embedded in the wall of the Regency House. But later, some of the ladies of the town said it was indecent, and the plaque had been removed and the opening was covered by a sign advertising Barling's Beer.

Mom Lanfield said, 'Isn't often that a man holds a door for me and tips his hat at the same time.' She winked at Link Johnson. 'Don't tell me we're getting culture in this place.'

Doyle started out the door, and Mom Lanfield said, 'I've never seen you over at my place.'

'No, that's right,' he said pleasantly, and went outside.

When he had gone, the Lanfield woman went to the counter, and handed Johnson a list of some of the things she wanted. 'Now that Kermit Doyle is the kind of a man I wish I'd met twenty years ago.'

'How many years, Mom?' Johnson said with a grin.

'Well, make it thirty then,' she said, and grinned back at him. Then she grew thoughtful. 'If that Sabrina Hale had any brains she'd cut loose from Sid Gunwright and marry Doyle. From what I hear they were pretty sweet before Doyle went to jail.'

'There's nothing wrong with Gunwright,' Johnson said carefully, remembering that for years Gunwright had been a regular patron of the Lanfield establishment.

'I had a little blonde once. Got her special for Gunwright. He used to treat her awful. Beat her up a dozen times. She was always black and blue.' Mom Lanfield sighed. 'I told her she didn't have to take that, but she was money-hungry, that kid.'

'That so?' Link Johnson said, and his opinion of Gunwright, already low, went down another degree.

'Know what happened to her?' Mom Lanfield was enjoying herself. 'Well, last year when I took that trip to St. Louis, I visited my sister. 'Course she thinks I'm running a boarding house. Well, anyhow, we go to a classy hotel and there coming across the lobby all plumed and diamonded is this blonde with a handsome gent. I ask my sister and she says they're married.' Mom Lanfield started to laugh. 'Remember that chunk of stone they had with my name on it at the Regency House?'

'Sure.' Link Johnson was interested.

'Well, there's an ad for Barling's Beer on it, isn't there?'

Johnson nodded.

Mom Lanfield was laughing so hard the tears rolled down her cheeks. 'Well, this blonde had married the heir to the Barling Beer outfit. So whether this damn town knows it or not, they're still advertising one of my girls at the Regency.'

Link Johnson started to laugh until he remembered suddenly that his wife had been one of a committee who had urged that the plaque honoring Mom Lanfield be taken down.

He turned to fill Mom's order.

CHAPTER TEN

Doyle spent the rest of the afternoon on the porch of the Regency, waiting for the first glimpse of Malgren, should the Skull Bar rider appear in town. He wanted the man for himself. It was really his fight, not the Barlows'. And if there were to be a showdown, he wanted witnesses. Not everyone in town was against him. At least, if either Pellman or Johnson saw the battle, they could give an accurate account to the sheriff. This way was better than waiting for Malgren to shoot him in the back.

At sundown, he went into the hotel for his supper and saw the Barlows at a rear table. Ellie was rigid in her chair. There was a fire and a sweetness about her that he had not noticed before. Doyle nodded, but none of

109

the Barlows returned the greeting. He took a corner table and he was aware that Ellie occasionally peered at him from the corners of her dark blue eyes.

Once old Jeb barked, 'Eat your supper, Ellie. Ain't nothing around here for you to look at!'

When they moved out of the dining room, Doyle did not even look up from his steak. Trying to be civil would be a sign of weakness in the eyes of the Barlows.

Neither were there any friendly nods from the other diners. They gave him a wide berth, and he could not blame them.

When he returned to the porch, it lay deep in shadow. He felt an increasing weight of depression. Somehow, seeing Ellie again had dampened his desire to settle the issue with Hamp Malgren. He could fight with a gun, but he was no gunfighter. He hated killing—and it could be that Malgren would kill him.

From the porch rail he looked at the stars, low in the cloudy sky. He turned his gaze to the east where the hint of a moon hung over the Temple Hills. The sound of piano music and a girl's brittle laughter came from a side street, and it reminded him that it was his second night of freedom, and he'd failed to make the most of it. The piano music was louder now. Mom Lanfield's was getting an early start.

He wondered if the girls would miss those 'regulars' who one day soon might die in the flame that would sweep the country. For it was building up. He could feel it, just as if he were riding through the woods in the darkness on patrol, knowing the enemy was ahead, sensing the sudden blast of orange flame from the thickets before it came. The prospect sickened him.

In one way this was a senseless fight, but he was part of it. The Skull Bar could buy guns; the hill ranchers were not warriors. And today he had not liked the implication of Harvey Brome's conference with Gunwright at Pellman's bar.

He turned his head, staring at the far end of Primrose Street, where he could see the glowing windows of Sabrina's house through the poplars. Maybe he was a fool, he told himself. What was a man's pride? So a woman such as Sabrina was not constant in her affections. Did it prove anything? Was her guilt any deeper than that of the husbands who occasionally rode to town for a 'game with the boys,' and instead joined drunkenly in song around the piano at the big house at the end of Chavez Alley, before going upstairs.

Then he saw her come along the walk, leaning intimately on Sid Gunwright's big arm. Suddenly it came to him how he could wound Gunwright deeper than any bullet.

When they climbed the steps together, Doyle removed his hat and stood against the porch rail.

Sabrina's eyes widened when she saw him and it seemed that she clung to Gunwright's arm with desperation. She said nothing, but Gunwright nodded. 'Good evening, Doyle.'

He watched them enter the hotel, Sabrina's back straight in a gray dress with black lace about the collar. Just before they found a table at the window, she looked back at him.

He went down the steps to the walk and was surprised to find Ellie Barlow standing in the darkness, holding a bolt of unwrapped yard goods. In the six months before his arrest he had never spoken to her; not until the day she had been so terribly frightened of Hamp Malgren. And he had been surprised at her speech. She did not talk like Jeb and her brothers. But then one day he learned that her mother had once been a school teacher.

Ellie said, looking toward the hotel dining room, 'I didn't think you'd still love her. Not after the way she treated you.'

He was surprised both at her statement and the vehemence in her voice. 'What makes you think I still care about her?'

'I saw the way you watched her,' Ellie said, and hugged the bolt of cloth tight against her bosom. 'I'm sorry. It's none of my business.' Then she gave a start and looked beyond him.

He turned, seeing the Barlow wagon in

front of Pellman's.

'Before Dad and my brothers come out, I want you to know that I appreciate what you did for me—that day. I've never had a chance to see you alone. And I couldn't express my thanks in front of Dad.'

'He should be more understanding.'

She sighed. 'He's an embittered man. He seems to think that he and the boys personally lost the war. Sometimes I think he enjoys finding someone to hate.'

Doyle sensed her loneliness, the hunger for affection that was denied her, living as she did with her father and brothers in the tight seclusion of the hills.

'Some day your father will learn, as I did,' Doyle said gently, 'that the color of a man's uniform is no guarantee of his character.' Then he added, 'A lot of people lost the war. The Barlows had no monopoly on it.'

She gave him a quick smile. 'Thank you for saying that.'

Then the three Barlows came out of Pellman's and stood beside the wagon staring down the walk at them.

Ellie stiffened. 'Now they'll be angered that I talked to you.' She hurried down the walk and old Jeb said something to her. The girl climbed into the wagon. Her father and brothers remained as they were for a moment, and although Doyle could not see their faces, he knew they hated him probably even more

113

than before.

He watched the wagon and the two riders move slowly out of town.

After making another tour of the town, Doyle was convinced that Malgren would not appear this night. He returned to the hotel, intending to get his buckskin. But as he passed an alley, he heard Sabrina call his name from a narrow slot between the buildings.

He turned, hand on his gun. If it were a trap, it was well concealed. He stepped up close to her, aware of her perfume.

'You've got to leave, Kermit,' she said in a breathless voice. 'Sid is a generous man. I had a talk with him, and he's agreed to write another check if you'll sign a quit claim deed.' She watched his shadowed face. 'Sid is waiting in the hotel. I told him I'd find you—'

'I think even less of him now than I did before,' Doyle said coldly, 'letting a woman run his messages.'

Her voice was frantic and angered. 'Can't you understand that you're a dead man if you don't clear out of this country?'

'Why should you care?' he said. 'You're going to marry Gunwright.'

'Yes, I am.' She touched his arm. 'You've got to understand this, Kermit. I'm different from most women. Maybe I'm hard, without a soul.'

Doyle gave a short laugh. 'Gunwright
114

hasn't married you yet.'

She was furious with him. Her body stirred restlessly so that he could hear the faint rustle of her skirts. 'Sid was very angry with you when he learned Slim Dorn was killed.'

'He was trespassing,' Doyle reminded her. 'But I didn't enjoy watching Dorn die.'

She bit her lip. 'I can see you're not going to accept Sid's offer.'

'No.'

For a moment she was silent. Then she said, 'I know I don't deserve a favor from you. But please destroy that trunk at Cross L. I don't think it's ever been opened.' Her voice lowered, and he knew she was truly afraid. 'My clothes couldn't have been found. Otherwise Sid would—' She didn't finish the sentence.

'You like money, Sabrina. What if Gunwright loses this fight? The Skull Bar would be broke.'

'He won't lose,' she said a little desperately. 'Because he's my kind.' Her voice was heavy with irony. 'Our kind never lose. Sid and I are heartless, without conscience.'

'Gunwright, perhaps. I'm not so sure about you.'

She seemed eager to prove her point. 'I deserted you, Kermit. I turned to Sid when you were jailed.'

Doyle watched as two men came out of

115

Pellman's, boarded their horses and rode leisurely out of town, the inevitable pall of dust settling behind them.

'Try to understand,' she said. 'I saw what fear of poverty did to my father—'

'You have a fair income from Copperjack stocks,' Doyle reminded her.

'But how long will it last?' She shrugged helplessly. 'Even if it should continue it isn't money enough for the way I like to live—the way I'm used to living.'

He was torn between disgust and pity. 'You plan to marry Gunwright, yet you were willing to meet me in Denver.'

She pressed a hand against her eyes and for a moment seemed to be fighting some inner emotion that was shaking her. 'If I were a foolish woman,' she said, peering at him from around her forearm, 'I'd run off with you, Kermit. But I have my future planned.' Her voice hardened. 'I've seen what this country did to my mother. She died before her time.'

He gave her a bitter smile. 'I can see now that you'd have been a little cramped living as my wife at Cross L.'

'I never intended living there. I intended once we were married for us to go to San Francisco. At that time I had enough money to set you up in a respectable business—'

'And far enough away so Gunwright couldn't reach you.' He shook his head. 'You don't know me very well if you thought I'd live on your money.'

'Then consider yourself lucky,' she said, 'that we never married.'

'I think I do.'

She stared at him, and he could see that her eyes were wet. 'Now you can take Sid's offer or not, just as you wish. You mean nothing to me. Absolutely nothing!'

She turned down the walk but she had not taken half a dozen steps when she flung an arm across her face and ran blindly into the hotel.

CHAPTER ELEVEN

Pete Tasker expected to have some trouble locating Kermit Doyle. But luckily the man had been pointed out to him on the street when he'd ridden to town earlier on another errand for Skull Bar, so he didn't have to depend entirely on Hamp Malgren's description of the man. Tasker walked his horse slowly up one side of the street and down the other. At last he spotted Doyle beside the hotel, talking to Sabrina Hale. This puzzled Tasker, because he'd heard that the boss was marrying the Hale woman and he couldn't understand why she should now be in such earnest conversation with an avowed enemy of the Skull Bar. Quickly

Tasker moved down the street into the shadows and waited, rolling a cigarette and lighting it.

Just thinking of Sabrina put a feeling of contentment in him. She was the kind of woman a man dreamed about when he lay in his bedroll of a night. He had seen her face many times, in the stars. A thin anger touched him and some of the things Gunwright had said and done came back and rubbed against his grain. But the real gall was the knowledge that Gunwright would take this woman for his wife. She was much too good for that proddy bastard. She should belong to a Texas man.

He saw Sabrina hurry into the hotel and Doyle start moving along the walk. Tasker mounted his horse and kept to the alleys out of sight. It wasn't long before he saw Doyle mount a buckskin horse, tied to the rack in front of the Regency, and ride slowly up the street.

Tasker waited in the shadows. The tall man on a buckskin came toward him, clearly outlined in the glare of the kerosene lamp at the entrance of Lipscomb's Livery.

Tasker spurred forward. Putting a note of anxiety in his voice, he said, 'Mister, have the Barlows got any friends in this town?'

Doyle reined in. 'I dunno,' he said suspiciously, staring at the lank rider. 'Why?'

Tasker jerked his thumb back along the

dark ribbon of road. 'Some of the Skull Bar crew jumped 'em about two miles east of town.'

Doyle was angered. 'You could have given them a hand,' he snapped.

'Hell, mister, I ain't horning in on any fight.'

Through Doyle's mind flashed a picture of Ellie out there somewhere, making a stand against the Skull Bar outfit at the side of her father and brothers. Silently he cursed Jeb Barlow for exposing his daughter to this danger. He considered telling the stranger to get word to Link Johnson and Pellman, but then realized that the two merchants could hardly be expected to take sides in a battle against Gunwright's men.

Without thanking the strange rider, Doyle wheeled the buckskin and spurred out of town, riding with his gun in his hand and straining to hear the first sounds of a gun fight. As he crested a ridge he saw that the moon had silvered the Flats so that the distant hills and the nearer brush-covered dunes were clearly outlined. Only to the north were clouds visible. Overhead the sky was clear. Again no rain.

Not more than a mile from town, where the road dipped through a nest of giant boulders, a noose sailed out of the air and caught him roughly about the arms. In the sudden pull of the rope he lost his gun and barely managed

119

to kick free of the stirrups. He struck the road heavily, momentarily stunned. When he tried to sit up, someone kicked him in the chest, and he fell back. He breathed with difficulty and he was seized with a touch of vertigo.

Then he winced as Hamp Malgren's laughter reached through the cottony thickness of his mind. 'So you're still fighting the Barlow battles,' Malgren said. 'Gunwright figured if everything else failed to budge you, to say that the Barlows needed help. When I seen them come by a while ago it gave me an idea.'

Doyle opened his eyes. There were two men with Malgren, and so far as he knew he had seen neither of them before. In a moment there was a pound of hoofs and the rider who had shouted the grim news that the Barlows were in a fight, dropped off his horse. The tall Texan came forward and peered down.

'So this is the famous Doyle,' Peter Tasker said. 'Let's get him to Skull Bar—'

'He ain't going there,' Malgren said. 'We're killing him—here.'

The three men looked at Malgren, then at each other. 'You sure that's the way Gunwright wants it?' Tasker said at last.

Malgren shook his dark head like an eager boy about to commit some mischief. The pit of Doyle's stomach turned cold. In the light of the match Malgren struck to fire up a cigar, his small eyes appeared yellow and insane. 'We're going to have fun with this one,' Malgren said. 'He crippled me up.'

'I should have killed you when I had the chance,' Doyle said.

'You're killing nobody,' Malgren said, and drew back his foot. Although Doyle managed to jerk aside, the toe of Malgren's boot ripped open his cheek. Then Malgren snarled, 'Why didn't you take Gunwright's eight hundred dollars, damn you! I sit out here waiting for you, but you got no money.'

Doyle felt Malgren search him in the hope that he might have taken Gunwright's offer at the last moment. He wondered if Malgren would kick him again. The fall had jarred him, and his head pounded. Blood from his cut face dripped down the front of his shirt. But he was not too far gone to realize Gunwright's plan—to give him a check for eight hundred dollars, have him cash it at the bank, and then let Malgren take it away from him.

With the rope still about his arms, Doyle was helpless. He began to catalogue his chances, and they did not look too promising. He saw Malgren sink to his heels, the cigar clenched in his teeth, and from the aroma he knew it was one Gunwright had given him.

'You kin to them Barlows?' Malgren demanded. 'Why else you come running every time one of 'em gets in a tight?'

121

'I just didn't want you to get your dirty hands on Ellie again,' Doyle said recklessly.

Instead of becoming angered, Malgren turned to his three silent companions. 'This here is a real tough man. Hold the rope, boys, and I'll see if he's so tough he's got buffalo hide for skin.'

Doyle struggled, but the rope was jerked tight and he found his shoulder blades in the soft road dust. He felt cold sweat on his back as Malgren straddled him and jerked open the front of his shirt and underwear. Malgren took a deep drag on the cigar so that the end glowed. Then he suddenly pressed the lighted end against Doyle's chest. For only a moment could Doyle steel himself. Then he cried out in pain.

Malgren got to his feet. 'What'd I tell you? He ain't so tough.' He stood looking down while Doyle felt nausea strike him from the ugly burn on his chest.

Malgren extended a hand to Pete Tasker. 'Give me your knife, Pete.'

Tasker asked, 'What you aim to do with it?' He seemed a little shocked.

'You'll see,' Malgren answered confidently.

Doyle felt the sickness spread through him when he saw Tasker hesitate a moment, then pull a knife from his belt and hand it over.

Malgren ran a thumb along the blade. 'You shot me in the back,' he reminded the man on the ground.

Doyle took a gamble, knowing it was his only chance. 'Do your friends know why I shot you?' he demanded.

'Never no mind about that,' Malgren said too quickly, and Doyle sat up. The front of his underwear touching the burned place set fire to his chest, but Doyle managed a tight smile. In the moonlight he could see the wicked scar on Malgren's forehead, his flaring nostrils, the small angry mouth.

'Maybe some of Gunwright's new riders don't know the kind of a man they bunk with,' Doyle said. 'You caught a girl out alone in the hills. And when I heard her scream, I rode up and shot you.'

'Shut up!' Malgren screamed.

But Pete Tasker said, 'Let him finish it.'

'She was just a kid, Malgren,' Doyle went on, 'but she fought like a cat.' His voice trailed off, and even then he wondered why Malgren did not plunge the knife blade into his breast. But the brutishly handsome face was perplexed, as if Malgren's slow mind could not react to this verbal attack.

Doyle felt the rope slack off around his arms as the three Skull Bar men looked at Malgren and shifted their feet in the dust. Doyle sensed his advantage, momentary as it might be, and pressed it.

'You're a big man against a defenseless girl,' he said scornfully. 'But how tough are you against a man? Supposing you and I settle

123

it with our fists?'

Malgren hesitated, then his voice was almost a whine. 'I'm crippled. How can I fist fight?'

'Then with a gun—if you've got the guts.'

Pete Tasker was of slighter build than Malgren and shorter, but he did not lack nerve. 'I ain't yet heard you call him a liar about the girl,' he said to Malgren.

While they were attentive on Malgren, Doyle got cautiously to his feet. And no sooner had he regained them than Malgren suddenly cried out in high-pitched rage and lunged at him. Instinctively Doyle wheeled, and the knife blade only ripped viciously into the slack of his shirt.

Before Malgren could pivot, the stocky Charlie Prince said, 'I don't hold for working on a man with a knife.'

The voice reached Malgren. He hesitated, breathing heavily. But only for an instant. He started for Doyle again, but Al Miller shoved him aside. 'Put up the knife,' he warned. 'If Gunwright wants him dead, a gun will do the job.'

Malgren handed the knife back to Tasker, then seemed to sense he had to redeem himself in front of these men. He started striking matches, peering at the ground. Finally the match glow revealed Doyle's gun where it had fallen to the road. He came back and laid the revolver on a flat rock.

'Walk over there and pick it up,' Malgren said. 'When you touch it, Doyle, I'm going to shoot your head off. You owe me a little edge because of this arm.'

Doyle heard the breeze stirring along the brushy dunes. The moon was bright, the stars were clean, and the air was warm. It was a hell of a night to die.

'You're a fine sport,' Doyle said thinly. 'It's your left arm that's stiff. Not your right.'

Then Malgren seemed to regain his confidence, or perhaps it was to shift attention away from his stiffened arm. His shrill voice seemed possessed of its usual bravado: 'If you want to know the truth, boys, it was me that catched Doyle with Ellie Barlow. And he tried to kill me so I wouldn't tell on him.'

'You're a liar,' Doyle said quietly.

Malgren stiffened. 'Go on and pick up that gun,' he ordered.

With one hand Doyle loosened the noose and drew it over his head and let it fall. His heart was pounding. In the distance he could see the lights of Regency glowing against the night sky. They'd probably kill him, he knew, but he'd make sure of one thing. He'd live long enough to get Malgren. He'd make sure that Malgren would never again find a woman alone in the hills.

He took a step toward the gun, then halted when a sharp feminine voice called from the shadows, 'Get your hands up, Malgren! And the rest of you! Lift them! High! Now!'

The men turned rigid and because the voice was behind them, they looked awkward and a little foolish. Slowly they turned and Doyle saw Ellie Barlow's slender figure moving into the moonlight from a brush-screened boulder. She held a rifle loosely so that she could easily shift her aim. 'You get it first, Malgren,' she warned. 'In the stomach. I promise you that. So don't make a move.'

In that moment Doyle stepped away from the four men and, before they could recover from their surprise, picked up the revolver Malgren had placed on the rock.

He cocked the revolver and said, 'Call off your boys, Hamp, or you're dead.'

CHAPTER TWELVE

The four men stood with hands raised, but Doyle wasn't sure they wouldn't do some crazy thing to endanger the girl. Malgren was raging, his voice shrill and uncontrolled. 'Don't let Doyle and the girl bluff you!' he cried, but made no move toward his belt gun.

The tall Texan, Pete Tasker, said in that quiet way of his, 'No need to worry, ma'am.' Then he looked at Malgren. 'I've had enough of you and enough of Skull Bar. I'm sick to my stomach.'

He unbuckled his gunbelt and let it drop. After hesitating only a moment his two companions, Charlie Prince and Al Miller, followed his lead. At last, Malgren reluctantly unstrapped his own gun harness, cursing as he did so.

When the gun dropped to the ground, Doyle stepped forward and struck him a hard blow in the face. Malgren spun, holding his bleeding face in his hands. His eyes that looked out through spread fingers were small and venomous.

'Pick up your gun, Hamp,' Doyle said.

Malgren didn't move.

'Either pick up the gun or tell Ellie you're sorry for what you tried to do that day in the hills.'

Doyle felt disgust that he sensed was shared by the three silent men. At last, Malgren smeared the blood off his face. He looked at Ellie. 'I—I'm sorry,' he mumbled.

'See if they're packing rifles, Ellie,' Doyle said, and she slipped into the shadows to the spot where they had left their horses. The mounts stirred restlessly. In a moment she returned with four Winchesters.

'Get on your horse, Hamp,' Doyle ordered. 'Next time I see your face I'll put a bullet in it.'

Without trying to press his luck further,

Malgren wheeled his horse and went spurring off into the darkness. The sounds of his horse were fading rapidly when Doyle turned to the three Texans. 'I'll leave your guns at the Temple Hills Junction,' he said.

'Fair enough,' Pete Tasker said, and looked toward Ellie standing with head thrown back, the rifle under her right arm. Tasker tipped his hat. Then the three of them mounted and rode slowly, but not in the direction Malgren had gone.

Only when the silence was complete again did Doyle let down the hammer of the gun, aware that his legs were trembling. He holstered the weapon, then crossed to Ellie. In the moonlight she looked wild and beautiful, and just seeing her there with her hair loose and blowing in the breeze exhilarated him. Ellie had nerve, and more.

'You're braver than most men,' he told her.

'No I'm not. I'm—' Her voice broke and she suddenly dropped the rifle and came against him, her arms clasped about his neck, her wet face against his cheek. 'I was scared,' she murmured. 'Oh, God, I was scared, Kermit.' Then she moved her head, and her mouth, wet and salty with her tears, was against his own. Gently he picked her up, carried her to the rock where Malgren had placed the revolver, and set her down. She had never called him Kermit before, and it made him feel uneasy.

'Where's Jeb and the boys?'

She dried her eyes on a forearm and sat with her hands clenched. It took her a long moment to speak. 'Dad was mad because he saw us talking together in Regency,' Ellie said. 'He kept at me all the way out of town. And when I said he should be proud to have you on our side, he back-handed me across the face—'

Doyle's mouth tightened.

'I made Dave give me his horse. I told them I was going to the hotel in Regency and if they ever wanted to see me again they could come and apologize.' She began to weep softly, but in a moment she sniffed back her tears. 'Then I saw these men in the road when I was riding back. I—I heard everything that was said. I'd have done something sooner,' she said as if apologizing, 'before they hurt you, but I had to wait until their backs were turned.'

'Jeb had no right to hit you.'

She shrugged. 'It isn't the first time. His heart is bad and up to now I haven't wanted to be the cause of him dropping dead when he was raging at me. But he's got to learn I'm not a chattel.'

Doyle stared off into the darkness. 'I should have killed Malgren when I had the chance.'

'And I'd have begged you not to, the same as I did that day in the hills. You could have

129

finished him then, but I asked you to let him go. And you did.' Her voice turned bitter: 'And as payment you were sent to jail and my name was ruined in this country.'

'Your name's not ruined.'

Her eyes were bright now. 'Stay away from Malgren. It's a Barlow fight. One day they'll find him alone. He'll pay. And somehow I can't help but feel a little sorry for him.'

He found his buckskin and caught up her roan. When they were mounted, she insisted on going to Regency, as had been her original intention, but he turned down the idea.

'Malgren isn't going to forget how you humiliated him tonight,' Doyle told her. 'He'll get drunk and—' He didn't finish. 'You belong at the Barlow ranch. I'll explain things to Jeb.'

'But they hate you!' she cried. 'You'll risk your life going there.'

'I've already risked it,' he said. 'Come on.'

He found Malgren's rope and strung on it the weapons he had taken from the Skull Bar bunch. Then he and Ellie headed east across the Flats, keeping to open country, for it was possible that Malgren had ridden to town for another gun or found other Skull Bar riders heading for Regency. But he sensed that Malgren would take a little time, before he acted, to think up a plausible story that would explain his failure to Gunwright.

In the distance Doyle could see a campfire,

130

and silhouetted against the glow, the figures of cattle. And he guessed that this was the Skull Bar cow camp. It was so very near the edge of Temple Hills, he noted, and felt a cold hand against his spine.

At the junction of the Regency road and the one that angled for the hills, Doyle left the weapons he had captured hanging on a mesquite. An hour later, when he and the girl reached the higher elevations, the night's heat was tempered by a cool breeze that carried with it the odor of lingering snows on the peaks of the Rubios.

It was ironic, Doyle thought, as they skirted a sand dune, that the vast and rich Skull Bar was starved for water, while the shirttail hill crowd had more than they could use. If Gunwright were a different man, they might all sit down and talk of throwing a dam across Dead Horse Canyon where Riondo Creek spilled down from the Rubios only to disappear under the basin sands. But you couldn't deal with Gunwright; the man would agree to no compromise. It was all or nothing with him. If the hill crowd appeased him once, he would make new demands and the bloody cycle would begin all over again.

It was well after midnight before they climbed the winding road that led to the Barlow place, situated on a knoll in the center of a narrow valley. Jeb Barlow had chosen his location for strategic reasons and here he could withstand a long siege behind the thick walls of his house.

At the crest of the hill the land flattened out and Doyle opened the weight and pulley gate. It squealed on unoiled hinges that would announce their arrival to those in the house beyond the aspens. As they rode across the dark and silent yard, Jeb Barlow's old voice cracked out from a corner of the house. 'Who's out there?'

'It's me, Dad,' Ellie said and swung down. 'Kermit Doyle is with me.'

Jeb came across the yard, a lank, shadowy figure with a rifle in his hands. He looked at his daughter a moment and Doyle could swear there was embarrassment in the old man's manner. At last he said, a grudging shame in his voice, 'I never meant to hit you,' he said. 'I was aimin' to send Dave to town for you tomorrow.' As if his apology had settled one issue he turned to Doyle. 'Step away from him, Ellie,' the old man said and lifted the rifle.

Painfully Doyle had slipped from the saddle. The burned place on his chest stung and his face ached from the raking of Malgren's boot toe. Now Ellie stepped in front of him. 'You've got to listen, Dad,' she told him. 'Malgren jumped Doyle—'

'Everybody expected that,' Jeb Barlow snarled. 'That ain't exactly news.'

But Ellie was persistent. 'Malgren had

three Skull Bar men with him, Dad.' She touched the old man on a thin arm and he drew back as if resenting this attempt to influence him. 'Do you know why Doyle left Regency and ran into Malgren's trap?'

'No, and I don't give a damn.' Jeb glared at Doyle from under the brim of his ancient hat.

Quickly she told her father how Kermit Doyle had fallen for Malgren's trick, thinking it was the Barlows who were being attacked by Skull Bar. 'He risked his own neck,' Ellie said furiously, 'because he thought we were in trouble.' She gave a bitter laugh. 'Can't you understand that every man in this country isn't your enemy?'

Slowly the old man lowered his rifle. He stared at the ground, as if trying to make up his mind about something. At that moment Dave Barlow appeared at the corner of the house, a lantern in one hand, a gun in the other. He had evidently overheard his sister's explanation of what had happened, for there seemed to be a lack of the usual malice in his eyes. He came up, and the volatile Curt joined him.

Curt said scornfully, 'I still don't like Doyle.' He looked at Doyle and spat on the ground, narrowly missing the toe of Doyle's boot.

Wearily Jeb Barlow waved a bony arm to shut up his son. He debated a moment, peering at Doyle, then he said, 'All right, so you thought you were helpin' the Barlows tonight. Which proves you ain't got as much sense as I give you credit for.'

'Dad!' Ellie protested angrily.

Jeb seemed a little cowed at the tone of his daughter's voice. 'Well, anyhow, Doyle, you should've killed Malgren. Might be you won't have him boxed again.'

'How can you kill a man,' Doyle asked, 'who won't even pick up a gun?'

'You tromp a snake, don't you?' The old man was staring at the gash on Doyle's cheek made by Malgren's boot. 'They was rough on you.' His voice softened a little and he turned his head. 'Go get some arnica, Ellie. And you,' he barked at his sons, 'get back to bed.'

When the three of them moved off to the big house, Jeb Barlow said, 'I don't like you much better'n Curt does. But I'll do a lot to stop talk about my gal.'

'It'll stop,' Doyle vowed.

But the old man was so engrossed in what he considered to be a solution to a perplexing problem that he appeared not to hear. 'You're welcome to stay here till we ride over to Canton for the meetin'.' He rubbed his chin thoughtfully for a moment. 'I could get word to Regency for that preacher to come out here—'

Doyle stiffened. 'I want the friendship of the Barlows,' he said, 'but hardly on those terms.'

134

It was like a blow in the face to Jeb and he stepped back and lifted his rifle. Dave and Curt, who had reached the side of the house, turned to look back at them for old Jeb had screamed a curse.

'You give my gal a bad name, Doyle!' Jeb Barlow cried. 'I was willin' to see her marry a man I don't like—'

'It was Malgren that gave her the bad name,' Doyle reminded the old man. And he felt his nerves tighten, for it was possible that this crazy old hill man would shoot him down in his tracks.

'We'll get Malgren,' Jeb said in that same cold, deadly voice. Even in the darkness his eyes seemed to glow with his meanness. 'And he knows it. Every day that son lives he's sweatin' because he knows that we'll find him some day—alone.'

A show of fear in front of this old hellion would spell his finish, Doyle knew, so he took the offensive. 'You've caused your daughter enough trouble,' he snapped. He felt miserable. His face ached, and the burn on his chest was a spot of unholy fire. He no longer cared what the Barlows thought. Curt and Dave, who were now coming back across the yard, and the old man could make of his talk whatever they pleased.

Jeb Barlow was trembling with anger. 'I don't believe neither story, yours or Malgren's.' He bared his crooked teeth, and

135

flung out his hands to block the advance of his two sons who flanked him. 'You clear out, Doyle,' Jeb said. 'Or my boys will cut you down.'

Curt said, 'You ever talk to Ellie again, and you'll wish you was dead!'

Wearily Doyle pulled himself into the saddle of the buckskin. 'If we can't stick together any better than this,' he told them, 'Gunwright will have us all hanging out on the fence to dry.'

He lifted a hand to Ellie who had come out the back door. Then he rode across the clearing. Until he was hidden by the barn he wasn't sure that one of them wouldn't shoot him in the back.

CHAPTER THIRTEEN

At the headquarters of the Skull Bar, Sid Gunwright leaned a thick arm on the mantel above the big stone fireplace that took up one corner of the parlor. As usual he was well-dressed, wearing a whipcord jacket and matching pants. His boots were polished. He looked better than he had yesterday at the cow camp or when he had ridden in to confront Sabrina. He held a full shot glass in one hand, staring at the amber liquid that was even with the rim of the glass. He was satisfied that his hand did not tremble so as to spill the whisky. He had come out from Regency this morning only to get bad news from Hamp Malgren.

The rider stood, hat in hand, conscious of his bruised mouth where Doyle had struck him. 'I had him cold, Gunwright,' Malgren said. 'But them damn Texans ratted on me and then the Barlow girl shows up—'

Clyde Fengean sat on a corner of a heavy plank table, smoking his pipe. 'Pete Tasker and his two friends don't seem like the kind who'd get scared and run,' he cut in.

'How about that, Hamp?' Gunwright said.

'They was scared of Doyle from the start,' Malgren said.

Fengean gave a short laugh. 'You ever see a Texas man run from trouble?' He fingered his short black beard.

Gunwright's fingers gripped the shot glass tighter. 'All right, Hamp,' Gunwright said. 'You can go now.'

When the rider had left, Fengean said, 'The sign's there, Sid. Read it. Those Texans just got sick of Malgren.'

Gunwright's gray eyes were angered. 'And if those Texans have got any sense, they'll clear out of the country.' He pondered a moment, scowling blackly through the window where he could see his whitewashed barns and corrals. 'Give orders to shoot them if they're seen on Skull Bar property.'

137

Fengean rose from the table, his heavy body stiffly erect on his short legs. 'I don't savvy you, Sid. You're letting this Doyle business wreck you.' When Gunwright made no reply, the foreman went on, 'You let three good men go and keep Malgren on. It don't make sense.'

'I've told you before,' said Gunwright, 'I'll use Malgren to bait the Barlows.'

He drained the shot glass at a gulp and wiped the back of a hand across his mouth. Too much had gone wrong. He wasn't used to defeat. He sensed a coolness on the part of Sabrina, and now he wondered just what she and Doyle had talked about last night on the street. She had entered the hotel crying. But it was his own suggestion that she have a try at getting him to sell out and she had seemed eager at the chance. Had she and Doyle talked about a quit claim deed or had they talked about something else?

He hurled the shot glass into the fireplace. It shattered against the stones.

Fengean watched him a moment, sucking on the stem of his scarred pipe. There was no pity in his eyes for this man he had seen grow from boyhood. 'Looks like rain this morning,' the foreman said. 'If we get rain, maybe we can forget about pushing into the hills. Maybe you won't need Doyle's ranch.'

Gunwright gave him an ugly look. 'Are you gutless, Clyde? Are you afraid of Doyle?'

Fengean rubbed the bowl of the pipe against his cheek, then stowed it in his pocket before he answered. 'I worked for your pa. Long as I draw Skull Bar pay I'll give you the same loyalty I give the old man.' His short beard seemed to bristle. 'But don't ever again call me gutless.'

Gunwright forced a smile to his frozen face. Of all things he wanted no trouble with Fengean. Gunwright's father had built up this ranch and then let it go to seed when he moved to town and lived off the money he had invested in Copperjack. He had left his son stock in the mine, which was now worth only a fraction of its former value. Gunwright got a grip on his temper. If he were to live in San Francisco with Sabrina in the style they both wanted, it was imperative that he grab off as many of the hill ranches as possible. Then, if there should be another drought, he would be insured against a lack of water.

'We've got the fight won, Clyde,' he told his foreman. 'And don't worry about Doyle. We'll handle him easily enough.' His tone gained confidence. 'And I fancy we might find one of the Barlows with a running iron in his gear.'

'These ain't the old days,' Fengean warned. 'There's law in this county now.'

Gunwright shrugged as if the law were of no importance. 'If one of my men should hang a Barlow, I'd naturally be angered. But after the deed was done there wouldn't be a damned thing Conodine could do about it.'

The side door opened and Skip Harlow entered. His old hat was tipped back so that a lock of gray hair curled over his forehead. He moved to the big table, limping because of the Mexican lead in his leg that he'd acquired when Gunwright's father and he had run off Mexican cattle. He leaned against the table.

'I'm quittin', Sid,' the old cook said.

Both Fengean and Gunwright gaped at him. Gunwright found his voice first. 'You'd better think it over, Skip. You're on a pension here, whether you know it or not. No other cow outfit would hire you to even rake manure.'

Skip Harlow turned red. Fengean walked over and put a hand on the cook's shoulder. 'What's eatin' you, Skip?'

'It's Malgren.'

'What about him?' Gunwright demanded.

'Some of the boys has got the idea that Malgren's runnin' Skull Bar, not you.'

'And if you've come to tell me that,' Gunwright said coldly, 'you can forget about quitting. You're fired. And if you ride a horse out of Skull Bar, you'll pay for it first.'

Skip Harlow took that without flinching, but his eyes got small and bright. 'I'm sayin' one thing before I go, Sonny.'

The 'Sonny' got Gunwright. He balled his fists and took a threatening step toward the

140

old man, then held himself in as Harlow began to talk.

'You ain't got one tenth the sense or nerve your dad had. Maybe he stole what he give you, but everybody was doin' it in them days, so who's to say what's right? He stole his first herd from the Mexicans. And I helped him. He come here and killed off any Indians that didn't like him movin' in. And I helped him. I swore to him the day he died that I'd help you. But I reckon even him, wherever he is, is sick of you now.'

'Clear out, Skip. Now!' Gunwright was livid. 'Don't bother to pick up a horse. Tell one of the boys to drive you to town. I don't want you riding anything with a Skull Bar brand.'

Skip Harlow gave him a twisted smile. 'Your boy, Hamp Malgren, is takin' hisself a nap in the boss wagon. Me and some of the other boys wondered what you figured to do about it.'

The old man turned on his heel and limped out the door, slamming it behind him.

Gunwright stood rigid. It was a law on Skull Bar that only any one of the cooks or the roustabout who cleaned up had access to the boss wagon. It was strictly what it was called. The wagon for the boss.

Fengean said, 'You lost three good riders in them Texans. You're going to lose a lot more if you let Skip Harlow leave Skull Bar. The

141

old-timers, including myself, remember he was your dad's best friend.'

Gunwright snorted.

But Fengean stepped around and faced him on his short legs, his chopped-off beard upthrust. 'And your pa meant for Skip to never do no hard work. He was to stay here the rest of his life. But you been sending him to cow camps. He's too old for that.'

'You want me to wrap him in lace and tuck him to bed?'

'You better do that, Sid.' Fengean took a hitch at his belt. 'You can buy riders for Skull Bar with money. But you can't buy loyalty.'

'And how about you, Clyde?' Gunwright said thinly. 'If Skip leaves will you follow him?'

'You let him get away from here and see.'

Gunwright had the hardest inner struggle of his life. He managed a grin, but the metallic hardness did not leave his gray eyes. He flung an arm across Fengean's shoulders. 'I'm tight strung, Clyde. I'm sorry I yelled at Skip. Of course he's not going to leave here.'

Then from a peg on the wall, Gunwright took down a shell belt and holstered revolver and buckled on the rig.

'A gun won't convince Skip to stay,' Fengean said.

'I'm not thinking of Skip,' Gunwright answered in a tight and deadly voice. He stalked outside and Fengean followed on his

142

short legs. It would give him a release to face Malgren. As he crossed the yard, he saw the crew, that portion working at the headquarters grounds, watching covertly. But first Gunwright jerked open the door of the long, tree-shaded bunkhouse. He stuck his head inside and yelled: 'Skip Harlow, if you try and leave Skull Bar, you're going to get your pants dusted with lead. Unpack that war-bag.'

He tried to make a joke of it. He laughed, and some of the men, because he was the boss, joined in. But Skip Harlow didn't laugh. Without words he mechanically started to lay out his stuff on his bunk again. Harlow hated to buckle under, but for forty years he'd been Skull Bar and he was a tired old man with Mexican lead in his leg and he knew he'd have to panhandle in Regency in order to eat. Now his pride was salved and much as he hated this pompous offspring of that old hellion he'd once ridden the Rio with, he knew where his only security lay.

'Thanks, Sid,' he said finally, but did not look at the man when he spoke.

Gunwright turned and went outside. The boss wagon was drawn up behind the corral. It had been driven in that morning by the six-mule hitch, a ponderous vehicle, ornate as a circus wagon. The crew watched him mount the steps and fling open the door. Inside Hamp Malgren lay on the big double bed, a

143

hat across his face to keep off the sun.

Gunwright caught him by an ankle, jerked him off the bed and to the floor. Malgren sat up in a welter of silken sheets, blinking, and reaching for the gun at his belt.

And because his inner tension was so great, Gunwright fervently hoped he would draw the gun. He wanted to spread Hamp Malgren all over the floor of the boss wagon. But Malgren, when he saw who it was, looked sheepish, and slowly got to his feet.

'Have you got special privileges around here, Hamp?' Gunwright demanded.

'No, I—'

'Then clear out of here. You're earning extra pay for special jobs. But that doesn't give you the right to sleep in my bed.' Gunwright stood aside as Malgren lurched outside and down the steps, glaring at the grinning crew. 'And if I catch you in here again, Hamp, I'm going to have the boys tie you to the fence and lay a wet saddle rope on your rump.'

Malgren jerked on his hat and shuffled off toward the bunkhouse to continue his nap.

At that moment a buckboard clattered into the yard, the yellow-haired Gorling handling the team. Gunwright crossed over. 'How's everything at Cross L?' he wanted to know.

Lew Gorling shrugged. 'All right, I reckon.' Then his gaze hardened. 'You fix Doyle yet?' he demanded thinly.

144

'Don't worry, we will,' Gunwright assured him.

'I ain't forgot it was him that turned them horses loose on Slim Dorn.'

Gorling had come in for supplies to take out to the Cross L. He started to drive toward the cookshack, then pulled up. 'O'Shane wants to know if you figure to keep any of Doyle's gear.'

'It's no use to me.' Gunwright laughed. 'And it won't be any use to Doyle. Burn it.'

'And how about the trunk?'

'I just got through telling you. Burn it.'

Gorling shrugged, but said, 'Seems a shame to burn up all them pretty clothes. Some gal would look mighty handsome in them.'

Gunwright went white. Fengean shot him an amused glance and said, 'What you know? Doyle was living out there with a woman.'

Gunwright tried to put a casual note in his voice. 'Would you say those clothes were expensive?'

'Well, all I know, I ain't never seen a gal dressed like that since I went to Queenie's parlor house in Cheyenne.'

Fengean emptied his pipe on his boot heel. 'Might be Ellie Barlow,' the foreman drawled. 'But she never had any expensive clothes that I ever saw. Who you figure it might be, Sid?'

Gunwright gave him a black glare, then turned to Gorling. 'On second thought, tell

O'Shane not to burn anything. I'll ride out and have a look at the stuff one of these days.'

Gunwright watched Gorling drive on down to the cookshack, then entered the house. With a shaking hand he poured himself a drink. Then he had another. There was the very devil in his eyes.

Slowly he began to pace the room. He traced out the pattern on a large red-and-black Indian rug on the floor. He wondered: How many of the crew besides Fengean guessed whose clothes they might be?

CHAPTER FOURTEEN

When Doyle woke after a restless sleep in the Temple Hills, there was the smell of rain in the air. Stiffly he got to his feet and stretched, seeing that clouds hung black and thick above the Rubios. He drew in his belt, for he had no food and his only chance would be a lucky shot at a rabbit. He was just contemplating this when he heard his buckskin nicker. He drew his revolver, peered around in the thick brush, but saw no sign of movement. Because he didn't want to be caught here on foot, he saddled his horse. He had just tightened the cinch when three riders appeared over a rim and started down a deer trail to his dry camp.

He cocked his gun and waited, recognizing the three men who had been with Malgren last night.

Warily he watched the lank Pete Tasker drop from a gelding. 'We got bacon and beans in a saddlebag,' Tasker drawled. 'You look like you could stand a bait of grub.'

Doyle shifted his gaze to Charlie Prince and the runty Al Miller. Both men had dismounted and were keeping their hands away from their guns.

'Last night,' Doyle said, 'you wanted to kill me. Now you want to feed me.'

'It was a job, that's all,' Tasker explained. 'I was already damn sick of Skull Bar and Clyde Fengean and Gunwright. Last night I got a whole lot sicker when I found out the kind of man I been bunking with.' He spat on the ground. 'Malgren!'

Still holding his gun, Doyle leaned against a cutbank. He owed these men one thing, at least. They had kept Malgren from using a knife on him.

Al Miller was bowed in the legs and had an oversize chin. He said, 'You hiring riders?'

Doyle laughed. 'I couldn't hire a jaybird to pick worms out of my yard, let alone gunmen.'

'We ain't gunmen,' the stocky Charlie Prince said. He had gray in his hair but he looked tough. 'But we ain't scared to do a little shooting.' He looked at Tasker who evidently was their spokesman. 'You tell him, Pete.'

'You got guts, Doyle,' Tasker said, as if he meant it. 'We'd admire to throw in with you.'

Doyle gave the trio a thin smile. They weren't much, just three riders you could find on any of a hundred ranches, with little to distinguish them from their brothers. Sun-hardened men who lived in the saddle, taciturn, giving grudgingly of their friendship. But although their offer seemed genuine enough, he had to consider the possibility that it was one of Gunwright's tricks.

'How'd you find my camp?'

'Spotted you from the ridge,' Tasker said. Then, as if sensing the doubt in Doyle's mind, he added, 'If Gunwright had sent us we could have potted you before you knew what hit you.'

Doyle rubbed his chin. He had to admit this was so. And it gave him a queasy feeling to know that Fengean or Malgren or Gunwright himself, for that matter, could have hammered a bullet into his backbone from the ridge.

'You boys from Texas?' Doyle said.

Pete Tasker nodded. 'But don't ask us why we left.'

'Nobody's asking.'

Doyle considered the three of them a moment. Texas, he thought. The Barlows

148

would like that.

'I see you found your guns,' he said.

'Yeah,' Tasker said, removing a tin of beans and a cloth-wrapped bacon end from his saddlebags. As if the matter were settled, Charlie Prince rustled wood and Al Miller tramped downslope to a creek for coffee water.

Later, Doyle balanced a tin plate on his lap, sitting with his back to a rock where he could watch them. The sun curled up over the hills, throwing its full heat into the canyon. Then clouds drifted in, and the temperature dropped quickly.

'Rain,' Doyle said hopefully.

Tasker nodded, munching a piece of bacon and looking at the sky. 'Beats all how the good Lord figures who he's goin' to favor. I 'member my poppa outa Austin raisin' truck garden. Well, we had a big rain. The cowmen was saved but it washed out Poppa's crop and he had to start over. He never did get back on his feet.'

'Poison for one is honey for another,' Doyle observed.

'And speaking of honey,' Peter Tasker said with reverence in his voice, 'did you see anything purtier than that Sabrina Hale? Why, if she'd just snap her pretty little ol' fingers I'd throw myself in a mud puddle and let her walk across my back.'

Doyle nodded soberly. 'She attracts

men,' he said. 'No mistake about that.' Then, because he wanted to change the subject, he said, 'If we win this fight, which is doubtful, I don't have much to offer you boys.'

Peter Tasker looked up from his plate, a touch of anger on his long-jawed Texas face. 'We ain't asked how much you got, Doyle. We already know. You got nothin'. Your cows are scattered to hellangone and the Skull Bar is using your place for a line shack. Well, me and the boys was run outa Texas because we bucked up against a big auger like Gunwright that had his strings laid clear to Austin. We was damn hungry when we took Gunwright's job. But we ain't that hungry now.' It was probably the longest speech the Texan had ever made in his life and he had to pause for breath before adding, 'You want us to side you or not?'

Doyle grinned. 'We can't camp out in the hills forever.' He looked at them. 'A man should be entitled to a decent bed of a night.'

Tasker's eyes brightened and he winked at Al Miller 'Go on, Doyle. What's on your mind?'

Doyle laid aside his empty plate. 'How long do you think it would take us to lay our blankets at Cross L?'

Pete Tasker winked broadly. 'I figure we could do it maybe by noon.'

'It's as good as done,' Doyle said, and ook each man by the hand.

150

When they got ready to ride, Tasker said, 'When I think of that Sabrina Hale going to marry Gunwright, I get sick. She is the purtiest woman I ever seen in my whole life. I'd saw off a leg just to kiss her fingers.'

'So would a lot of men,' Doyle said. 'And a lot of men have stroked a kitten and didn't realize they'd caught a bob cat until they counted the scratches on their arms.'

Tasker gave him an odd look. 'You don't like her for some reason?'

Doyle sensed a hardness in the lank man's voice, and tried to shrug it off. He had just found three men ready to join him in the fight against Skull Bar, with little or no remuneration at the end of it. And the whole project was threatened with disaster even before it got started. Because by now it was obvious to Doyle that Pete Tasker was in love with Sabrina.

'You said one thing that's true,' Doyle said, and grinned. 'She's the prettiest woman you'll see in a month's riding.'

'The purtiest a man will see in a lifetime,' the Texan said, softening a little.

They waited until they could hit the Cross L at noon, Tasker, Prince and Miller riding ahead to provide the element of surprise. Doyle was gambling on the possibility that the Skull Bar men at Cross L had not learned that the trio no longer worke Gunwright. It was their only chance.

151

crew probably outnumbered them.

From the aspen grove where he had watched Slim Dorn die, Doyle saw four Skull Bar men, who had been eating their noon meal, stumble from the house. They were irritated and cursing their luck, because Tasker had yelled something about an important message from Gunwright. But their irritation fled when they beheld the drawn guns of the Texans.

The fat Tim O'Shane looked shocked. 'What you doing, Pete?' the cook demanded. 'This a joke?'

'You're on private property, Tim,' Tasker informed him.

At that moment Doyle rode up. The Skull Bar men seemed unable to understand why Tasker and his companions had suddenly switched to Doyle. But as they recovered from their surprise, their eyes hardened. They had battled with Doyle. One of their number had been trampled to death by the panicked horse herd.

Doyle said, 'You've got half an hour to pack up and clear out.' He jerked his head at Al Miller. 'Get their guns.'

When the Skull Bar guns were quickly collected, Tim O'Shane still looked bewildered. 'We was supposed to wait here Fengean.'

sker grinned and nudged him in the ribs his revolver barrel. 'You go meet

Fengean,' the Texan said. 'It beats waiting for him.'

'I don't figure this,' O'Shane said, and looked toward the house where the men were swearing as they rolled up their blankets under the guns of Miller and Prince.

Tasker put a hand on Tim O'Shane's arm. 'You got a chance to get on the right side in this fight, Tim.'

Doyle, standing near Tasker, watching the road, added, 'You'll be doing us a favor, Tim.'

But O'Shane had a certain loyalty and the Skull Bar had been paying his salary. He licked his lips, then said, 'Reckon I'll stay with Skull Bar,' and stepped into the house to get his gear.

'That's the trouble with these things,' Tasker said a little sadly. 'There's always some nice fellas on the other side.'

'I know what you mean,' Doyle said grimly. 'That's one thing I learned in the war.'

The Skull Bar men were out of the house with ten minutes to spare, their gear loaded on pack horses. Just as they prepared to mount, the sounds of an approaching wagon could be heard down the canyon. Their surliness at being kicked out turned to hope, and Doyle knew they were considering the possibility that riders might be coming behind the wagon—Skull Bar men.

'Hold it,' Doyle warned them. 'First man that yells will get hurt.' He swung the Winchester he had taken from one of them, and they knew he meant what he said.

They sat silently in their saddles, unarmed, stiff with anger. Lew Gorling, hat tipped back on his shock of yellow hair, came swinging around a bend in the brush lined canyon, driving a loaded buckboard. For only a moment did the yellow-haired man seem frozen. Then he tried to snatch up a rifle from under the seat. As he straightened, Charlie Prince shot him. The shock of the bullet sent Gorling over the back of the seat into the bed. The team bolted, but Tasker and Miller crowded it against a bank and got it under control.

They got Gorling's belt gun and rifle and bandaged a hole in his shoulder. He seemed weak from shock, but he could still glare at Doyle. 'I ain't forgot Slim Dorn,' he said through his teeth.

'Neither have I,' Doyle said as he tightened the bandage.

What grub they needed they unloaded from the buckboard. 'Tell Gunwright it's part payment for the trouble he's caused,' Doyle told them.

Then he sent them on their way, one of the other Skull Bar men driving the rig, Gorling in the bed lying on a blanket.

Just before they disappeared around the

bend in the canyon, Tim O'Shane looked back and lifted a hand to Pete Tasker.

Tasker waved back. 'Kind of gives me the creeps,' he said soberly, 'thinking maybe I'll be looking at Tim over the snout of a gun.'

Doyle nodded. 'It's no fun.'

Tasker looked grim. 'I owe Tim four dollars for poker the other night, and he never even asked me for it.'

They went into the house and looked around. The place was clean enough, but the bunks built along one wall were crudely constructed and seemed to have been built with no thought of permanence.

'From here on out,' Doyle said, 'we sleep light and with a gun under the blanket.'

'Amen,' Pete Tasker said.

CHAPTER FIFTEEN

Because there might be other Skull Bar men in the hills who could join up with the group kicked off Cross L, Doyle decided to do some scouting. While the three Texans carried the captured supplies into the house, he rode off down the canyon. From a ridge he could see a spiral of dust and knew from the size that it marked the progress of the Skull Bar crew to headquarters. But to the left another and larger pall of dust hung against the cloudy sky. That, he reasoned, would be the Skull Bar herd Gunwright intended throwing into the Temple Hills.

To make sure, he cut along the top of the ridge, intending to get a closer view of the herd. But before he had gone a mile he saw below in the canyon, at the foot of a giant cottonwood tree, a rider sitting on a deadfall. A sorrel horse grazed nearby.

Doyle edged nearer, his buckskin crashing through the brush because there was no trail. The figure below looked up and now he saw that it was a girl. Doris Brome. Because he did not want to frighten her, he took off his hat and waved. She waved back. Then he cut down to the bottom of the canyon. She had laid her flat-crowned hat on the deadfall. In her boy's shirt and jeans she looked young and trim. Not as pretty as Ellie Barlow, but with a clean fresh look about her.

'You shouldn't be out here alone,' he said, thinking of Hamp Malgren.

'I know,' she said, and clasped her hands together. Her arms were tanned and her breasts nicely pointed against the front of her shirt. 'Curt and I often meet here. It's the only chance we have.'

Doyle swung down, trailed the reins and rolled a cigarette. 'Your mother still against you marrying him?'

'Yes. I love Curt and he loves me. But Momma—'

'What's your mother got against Curt?'

'Momma's brother died at Libby Prison. She thinks that every reb was responsible. That's why she hates the Barlows. I try to tell her that it was war then, but now it's supposed to be over.' She let her hands fall to her sides. 'It's wicked for people to hate like Momma hates.'

Doyle got his cigarette going. 'Your dad and mother don't get along very well, I take it.'

She looked at him in surprise. 'What makes you say that?'

He knew he had said too much, but he wanted to help this girl. He didn't think much of Curt Barlow, but if she loved the man ... 'Well, maybe if your mother got a little more love from your father, or gave a little more—' He was in deep water. He didn't think Doris Brome understood at all what he meant.

'I'm afraid of what will happen if Momma ever catches Curt and me together. Or Poppa, either, for that matter. He does whatever Momma says.'

'I'll wait here till Curt comes. Then you better have him ride you near enough home so you'll be all right.'

But the girl seemed not to hear him. She stood staring at the ground, her face pale. 'Momma hates this country. She wants to move away and it's only because of Curt. I'm

157

sure of it.'

Doyle felt grim, remembering Harvey Brome talking to Gunwright in Pellman's bar. He wanted to tell the girl that she didn't have to move away if she didn't want to, that if Curt were the man she seemed to think he was, Curt would marry her and keep her here. But he couldn't believe that she'd find any more happiness than Ellie had, living with the Barlow clan.

'Here comes Curt now,' Doris said, and brightened. She took a small white handkerchief from her pocket and dried her eyes. 'I don't want him to think I've been crying.'

Doyle watched Curt ride up the path that bordered Riondo Creek. He rode loosely in the saddle, lean, wide of shoulder. As usual his face was dark, immobile.

'Mr. Doyle's been keeping me company till you came,' Doris called to him.

'That so?' Curt swung down lightly. He walked past Doris, his head tilted a little to one side. And suddenly he struck Doyle in the face, reopening the cut on the cheek first put there by Hamp Malgren's boot.

Dazed, taken completely by surprise, Doyle fell backward and sat heavily on the ground. He shook his head, and felt blood coursing warmly across his cheek.

Doris was hanging onto Curt's arm, but he shook her off. 'Please, Curt—'

Curt came up and tried to kick Doyle in the face. But this time Doyle was ready. He twisted aside and caught Curt's swinging leg at the ankle. Curt toppled, throwing out his hands to break his fall. Doyle stood up, dabbing the back of a hand against his cut face.

'Are you Barlows all loco?' Doyle demanded.

Curt stayed on the ground a moment, then leaped to his feet and lifted his fists. Doyle stepped in, took a blow to the chin, but rocked Curt's head back with a solid smash. Curt caught him by the belt, lifted him and spilled him to the ground. They wrestled and Doris screamed. At last Doyle got on top. His fingers found Curt's throat and he banged the man's black head against the ground.

'You're making a fool out of yourself, Curt,' Doyle panted, 'in front of your girl.'

'You put your dirty hands on my sister. You ain't goin' to do it to Doris—'

Doyle came to his feet and picked up the gun that had dropped from his holster when Curt had first rushed him. He cocked the revolver and pointed it at Curt. Barlow had bruised lips, a tear over his right eye and the marks of Doyle's fingers still on his throat.

'I'm tired fooling with you, Curt,' Doyle said. 'You let Doris meet you out here when you know Malgren's still loose—' He wiped his mouth.

Doris had dropped to her knees beside Curt. 'Please believe this, Curt. Mr. Doyle meant no harm. He wanted to wait until you came and could ride me home—' her voice broke—'or nearly home.'

Curt Barlow got up, snatched his hat from the ground and beat out the dust on his knee.

'If you've got half the nerve I think you have,' Doyle said, 'you'll ride Doris all the way home and tell her folks you intend to marry her.'

Doris put her hands over her mouth and her eyes were wide with terror. 'I'm afraid to do that, Mr. Doyle. Momma—'

Doyle holstered his gun. He jerked his head at Curt. 'See you at the meeting tomorrow.'

'See you in hell,' Curt said.

Doris shook her head. 'Please, Curt. Don't be that way. He's only trying to be nice.'

Doyle mounted the buckskin and rode into the brush. He had a cold spot between his shoulder blades. For the second time in a matter of hours he wondered if one of the unpredictable Barlows would shoot him in the back. But no shot came from the ridge. He looked down. Curt and the girl sat close together on the deadfall and from their attitude he knew both of them were dejected. He wondered what old Jeb would say if he knew his youngest son was courting a Yankee girl. Probably spout fire through his nose,

160

Doyle thought, and paw the ground and go looking for Harvey Brome with a shotgun because the rancher had sired the girl.

Doyle turned his buckskin back to Cross L.

Whatever victory they had won at Cross L was only temporary, Doyle knew, for the Skull Bar's superior forces could regain their advantage at any time. But during the rest of the day and night, no attempt was made to attack the house. Doyle knew his only chance lay in having the hill crowd solidly behind him. Otherwise it was hopeless.

The following morning they saddled up. Although Doyle realized that to pull out was to invite Skull Bar to move in, he wouldn't leave the three men behind to run a risk he wasn't able to face himself. They cut west, along the old Copperjack road, deeply rutted from the wheels of the ore wagons, then up through Rifle Pass in the Rubios where the wind always howled. When he saw the sprawling copper mine in the valley below, Doyle thought of Sabrina and how the faltering ore vein had killed her father and driven her to Gunwright for security. It was a hell of a world, he mused, when the loss of a dollar would finish a man and cause his daughter to put herself on the block.

By the time they reached Canton the clouds had thickened until the sun was blotted from the mountainous country. There wasn't much to Canton, which consisted of a two-story combination hotel and saloon called Sprague's, and a blacksmith shop. When Doyle rode up with his three men he counted eight horses at the rail in front of Sprague's. They tied their horses and went inside.

Most of the ranchers had already arrived. The two Dunkle brothers, Emil and Bruce, looked up from the pool table where they were shooting a game with Bert Smalling and Lew Harper. When the men saw Doyle, they racked their cues and took chairs against the wall. Bert Smalling, ruddy-faced and quick with his temper, peered at Doyle's three new riders who were drinking beer at the bar.

'What are you up to, Doyle?' Smalling snapped. 'Them are Skull Bar men. Seen 'em myself last week with Gunwright in town.'

Patiently Doyle explained how the trio had decided to throw in with him. Smalling and the beefy Dunkle brothers were frankly skeptical. Lew Harper, a lean, sun-dried man, gray in the head and beard, solemnly shook Doyle's hand. 'If you vouch for them fellas,' he said, 'it's good enough for me.'

They sat drinking beer, discussing their chances in the grim business which lay ahead.

The success of what they termed the Temple Hills Pool depended upon one man. 'If Harvey Brome comes in,' Emil Dunkle said, 'then we're all right. If he don't—'

The men grew restless, waiting for Brome

and the Barlows to arrive. It was sultry in the barnlike saloon, and they continued drinking beer to pass the time. In each man was a reluctance to fight, Doyle knew. It was too soon after the war. Each of these men had come here and put down his roots and hoped to be let alone. None had figured on the drought or Sid Gunwright's insatiable ambition.

An aura of foreboding settled over Doyle and he went out to the veranda to get a breath of air. Pete Tasker followed him outside and the two of them stared glumly at the build-up of heavy clouds over the Rubio peaks. A horseman cut up through the junipers beyond the stage road and Doyle recognized the heavy, mustached figure of Dave Barlow. He was surprised to see the eldest Barlow brother alone.

Dave slid down from his horse, tied it and met Doyle on the veranda. 'You better stay out of Curt's way,' Dave said coldly. 'He says you horned in where you ain't wanted.' Then his eyes shifted to the red-haired Pete Tasker. 'Doyle, I hear you got yourself a crew.'

'Yeah,' Doyle said. He scanned the trees to see if the rest of the Barlows were coming. With Ellie, he hoped.

'Heard you run out the Skull Bar from your place,' Dave Barlow said.

'It's no guarantee they'll stay out,' Doyle said dryly. 'Where's the rest of the clan?'

Instead of answering, Dave shot him a withering glance and entered the saloon, spurs ringing on the plank floor. Puzzled by the new venom in the man's eyes, Doyle followed him in, trailed by Pete Tasker. The talk was general and no one seemed to want to discuss the business of the Temple Hills Pool until Harvey Brome arrived.

It was the middle of the afternoon before Harvey Brome entered Sprague's. He halted just inside the door, a certain fear in his eyes when he saw Dave. But Brome, after that moment of hesitation, strode forward and joined them. He shook hands all around, but Dave Barlow was busy with his bottle of beer and appeared not to notice his outstretched hand.

Doyle felt a tightening along his nerves.

Finally Bruce Dunkle said, 'Dave, where's Jeb and your brother?'

Dave seemed to ignore the question. He sat on the edge of the pool table, the center of his sickle mustache damp from the beer. 'I hear there was some trouble over at your place yesterday, Brome,' Dave said.

The harsh tone seemed to shrink Brome into his chair. To Doyle, the mild-mannered little man always seemed to be the type who should be clerking behind a counter instead of trying to eke out a living in the tough hill country.

Dave said, 'Curt come home with his face

all bloodied up.' His gaze slid to Doyle a moment, then back to the obviously frightened Brome. 'But damn if the rest of Curt ain't all cut to hell. Looks like somebody took a horsewhip to him. But Curt swears it ain't so.'

Lew Harper fingered his gray beard. Then he stepped between Dave and Harvey Brome. 'We're here to discuss the Temple Hills Pool—'

Dave slid off the edge of the pool table. 'And I come over here to tell you that the Barlows are going to fight it alone.' He looked grim as he added, 'Unless you get rid of Doyle.'

Kermit Doyle heard the sucked-in breath of the men, the quick exchange of glances, and felt his own face redden at the insult.

'If Doyle's in the pool,' Dave said, 'the Barlows are out!'

There was a buzz of talk from the ranchers. Emil Dunkle shifted his big body in the chair. 'Reckon this calls for a vote on you, Doyle.' He scowled, adding, 'There ain't nothing personal in this. I like you, but I hear Gunwright made you an offer.'

'And I turned it down.'

'This time, maybe,' Emil Dunkle said. 'But next time—' He spread his big hands.

His brother Bruce nodded. 'If the fight gets rough, you might pull out on us, Doyle. You're new around here, but the Barlows

165

been here long as most of the rest of us.'

Doyle said stiffly, 'I can leave now and save you the trouble of kicking me out.'

Bert Smalling snapped, 'Now that ain't no way to act, Doyle.'

'We'll take a vote,' Lew Harper said, and winked at Doyle to let him know that he would have at least one affirmative vote in this crowd. For a moment Doyle was tempted to explain the reason for the Barlow hatred, then thought, the hell with it. He knew the reasons, well enough. He had turned down Jeb's offer of marriage to his daughter. And Curt had further added fuel to the fire after the fight yesterday in front of Doris Brome. And behind that was the old business with Malgren.

Harvey Brome got unsteadily to his feet, his eyes downcast. 'I—I'm not voting,' he blurted. 'I just rode up to tell you that I—' He stopped. Then the words tumbled from his lips as if he had been eager to explain all along but until this moment had lacked the nerve. 'Gunwright bought me out.' Brome slumped back in his chair and refused to meet any of their eyes.

'I'll be damned,' Bert Smalling muttered.

'I got a family,' Brome said. 'I went through one of these things in New Mexico and it killed my first wife. I'm taking the money Gunwright give me and heading north. I—I just ain't cut out for this sort of

166

thing.' He got to his feet, and for a moment Doyle thought he would burst into tears. 'I'm sorry boys,' Brome said, and shuffled for the door, head down. They heard him ride out.

It was quite a while before anyone spoke. Then Emil Dunkle said, 'That gives Gunwright a big foot in our front door.'

'Can't blame a man too much when he's afraid for his wife and kids,' Lew Harper said dispiritedly.

'Never knowed Brome was married before,' Bruce Dunkle said.

Lew Harper nodded. 'Yeah, it was Doris' mother. Harvey married Agnes later and had the two boys by her.'

'That explains a lot of things,' Doyle said, more to himself than to these men. Perhaps that accounted for Agnes Brome's seeming hatred of Doris and her attempts to thwart her marriage plans under the guise of 'these terrible times.'

Bert Smalling ended all discussion of the Bromes. He flung a hand toward the front of the saloon. 'It's started to rain!' he shouted.

Drops the size of double cagles stained the dusty window panes. The men rushed to the door to stare in awe at the road that was rapidly taking on the appearance of a bog. It wasn't a rain. It was a cloudburst. Doyle jerked his head at Tasker and his companions and they started to leave.

'Where you going?' Lew Harper

demanded. 'We haven't taken that vote yet.'

'About the only thing we can vote on is a fitting epitaph for the Temple Hills Pool.' Doyle gave the mustached Dave Barlow a tight grin. 'With Gunwright on Harvey Brome's land, we haven't much chance, any way you look at it.' He added as a parting shot, 'You and the Barlows stick together. The Cross L will be the one to go it alone.'

They untied their slickers and shrugged into them, then boarded their horses. The four Cross L men rode away from Canton in the driving rain.

Later, Pete Tasker said, 'Now why would anybody take a horsewhip to a man?' Tasker scowled. 'Unless it's over some woman.'

'You've probably got it right, Pete,' Doyle said wearily. 'An angry woman with a whip can be dangerous to a man. Even somebody like Curt Barlow.'

CHAPTER SIXTEEN

Because Harvey Brome had willingly sold out, Gunwright seemed to be turning his attention to that end of the hill country. Doyle was thankful for the respite, but knew it was only temporary. He heard that Brome had a week to load up his household objects and clear out. During the nights at Cross L, when it was his turn to stand guard, Doyle thought of Sabrina, remembering the softness of her hair against his cheek, the frenetic passions hidden deep inside. Then his thoughts would turn to Ellie Barlow. Somehow, every time he went near the girl, he found a sense of peace amid trouble. A man would know where he stood with Ellie. But Sabrina...

Somehow, in spite of all the trouble the man had caused, he did owe something to Hamp Malgren. Save for that shooting over Ellie, he would now be the husband of Sabrina, a man owned and chained in hell. Me living in Frisco, he thought, on her money. The idea was amusing and at the same time pathetic. Sabrina had so wanted to be free of Gunwright. Or so it seemed. But now she was right back in his corral again.

That afternoon Clyde Fengean had thrown three-hundred-odd head of Skull Bar cows into the Temple Hills, four miles south of the Barlow headquarters. And the Barlows had quickly retaliated, shooting a dozen or more prime Skull Bar beef in the head. The Skull Bar foreman had announced that the next Barlow he found would be finished on the spot.

The war was on.

Doyle got the word from Harvey Brome who rode over at sundown, glum ar frightened. They sat on the steps w'

Brome recounted these tragic happenings.

Doyle said, 'Why does a man think he can go it alone in this world? With the pool we might have had some chance, but now—'

Harvey Brome looked sick. 'You blame me for selling out.'

'I don't blame you, Harvey. I know what you're up against.'

Brome seemed to take heart in this. 'Agnes is a good wife,' he said, 'but—'

'She's jealous of Doris. Because every time you look at Doris you think of your first wife.'

Brome nodded sadly. 'Reckon that's right.' He raised pathetic eyes to Doyle's face. 'I come over here for a special reason, Doyle. I—' He seemed to find it difficult to speak. 'Doris ain't been home. Her and Agnes had a powerful fight and Doris sneaked out at night. She hitched up the wagon and took a bottle of my best bourbon and a rifle.'

Doyle tried to sound confident. 'She's just trying to worry you.' He smiled. 'She'll come back.'

'I don't figure it that way, Doyle. I don't think she'll ever come home.'

'Did you try tracking the wagon?'

'I tracked it clean to Regency. I hunted all over town. Ain't nobody seen Doris. And I couldn't find the wagon either.'

'Maybe she took the stage.'

'No. Everybody in Regency knows Doris.

Somebody should have seen her.' He was pitiable, a little man caught in the big squeeze. A wife who hated his daughter by a first marriage on one side of him. The awful prospects of a range war on the other.

Doyle said, 'She'll turn up,' and wished he meant it.

Brome got to his feet from the porch steps. 'I'm scared, Doyle. Scared for Doris.' He licked his lips nervously. 'I can't help but remember the Barlow girl and Hamp Malgren. Doris out there alone—'

Because he wanted to lighten his burden, Doyle said that Malgren had undoubtedly learned his lesson and wouldn't try anything like that again. In this country, anyway.

'If you tracked the wagon to town, it probably means Doris is still there, staying with friends.' He gave Brome a sharp look. 'Or maybe the wagon was a decoy. Maybe she and Curt ran off.'

'I rode to the Barlow place,' Brome said heavily. 'Doris wasn't there. Reckon it was only old Jeb that kept Curt from shooting me. I—' He dug a hand into his pocket and pulled out a soiled and wrinkled envelope. 'Just about forgot this.' He added, embarrassment thickening his voice, 'Met Mom Lanfield in Regency. She said she's been looking for you. It's about the loan she made you to buy this place.' He handed over the letter. 'She says this will explain.'

It was on the tip of Doyle's tongue to call Mom Lanfield a lying old woman. But something cautioned him and he ripped open the letter.

Mr. Doyle:
Must see you on a matter of extreme importance. Come to rear door of my place. Tonight.
    Lanfield

Doyle stuck the letter in his pocket. 'Yeah, she did loan me some money.' He tried to grin, as if borrowing money from a woman like Mom Lanfield wasn't exactly the worst crime in the world. 'You go on home, Harvey. I'll go to Regency and while I'm there I'll see if I can get a line on Doris.'

'I'll go with you.'

Doyle shook his head. 'I still think Doris is probably meeting Curt somewhere.'

'I don't think so. Somehow Jeb learned about it. He said Curt wasn't going to marry any Yankee girl and that was final.' Brome sighed. 'In matters like that I figure old Jeb has the final word.'

'Don't be too sure,' Doyle said. He told Tasker and the others that he'd be back in the morning. Then he rode with Brome to where their trails branched.

It was there that Brome said, 'Find Doris. I—I swear I'll make Agnes treat her better.'

172

Doyle nodded, seeing Brome with his fists clenched. He knew how much chance Brome had of making his wife take a gentler view toward Doris. A pretty slim chance at best.

★   ★   ★

Instead of arriving in Regency by way of Primrose Street, Doyle turned west and cut among the abandoned houses and shacks and weed-grown lots at the far end of Copperjack Street. Using an alley between the boarded up buildings, he approached Mom Lanfield's place from the rear. There was nothing to indicate the type of establishment; just small windows in a low, frame building that stretched the length of a block at the north end of Chavez Alley. In the boom days the entire building had been used, but now only a quarter of it seemed occupied. Windows of the remainder of the structure were covered with heavy wooden shutters.

Looking carefully around to see that he was not observed, he tied his horse behind a shed and advanced on foot. It was not impossible that Gunwright had rigged a trap for him and in some manner persuaded Mom Lanfield to bait it. Whatever risks involved he would have to face. He knocked on the door and in a minute heard footsteps. A heavy bolt was withdrawn and the door opened a crack. It swung wider.

Mom Lanfield, wearing a black dress and strings of beads, a shade redder than her dyed hair, stood in the opening. 'So you got my note,' she said. 'I was afraid Brome might not deliver it.'

Doyle stepped into a narrow hallway, deeply shadowed because of curtained windows. 'Must be something important to get me all the way to town,' he said dryly.

'Doris Brome,' Mom Lanfield said, coming right to the point. She saw the surprise on Doyle's face and said, 'Doris is here.'

'*Here*?' He fairly shouted it and the Lanfield woman put a quick finger over her lips. 'Last night late I heard a knocking at this door and opened it. Doris had driven to town in her father's wagon. She had a bottle of whisky. Lord knows how much she'd drank. But she was hysterical. I didn't know what in the world to do with her—'

'Anybody else know she's here?'

Mom Lanfield shook her red head. 'No. But you know what gossips would do to Doris Brome if it ever got out that she was here. That's why I sent for you.'

'She asked for me?'

'In so many words,' the Lanfield woman said. 'She said you were the only person in this country who seemed to understand her. I took a chance when I saw Harvey Brome on the street, and sent that note to you.'

Doyle followed her to a small room with a

barred window that had once been used for storage. A cot had been moved in and Doris Brome lay on this, her eyes swollen almost shut. When she saw Doyle, she sat up on the cot, threw her arms about his waist and began to sob again. He felt very foolish and he pried her fingers loose and sat down on the edge of the cot.

'I can guess what happened,' Doyle said grimly. 'Your mother found you and Curt and took a whip to him.'

'Yes. She whipped him like a dog. And Curt and me were only saying goodnight. He was kissing me.' She began to sob again. 'Momma is hateful.' Doris Brome's eyes began to glow. 'Do you know what Momma called me?'

'No.'

'She called me a—' The girl's voice broke. 'I can't say it. I grabbed a bottle of Poppa's whisky. I wanted to drink and then come here. I wanted to be wicked like Momma said I was. I wanted Momma to know I was here—' Her voice trailed off as if she might not be so certain of her desires at the moment. 'The whisky made me sick.' She slumped back on the cot, weak from exhaustion.

Doyle looked at Mom Lanfield. 'Where's the wagon?'

'In an empty livery barn down the street put it there myself.'

'I'll be back soon as I can get it ready,' he said.

Outside the shadows were lengthening along Chavez Alley. Making sure he was not observed, he rode to the livery Mom Lanfield had indicated. It had once been a stable, but since the decay of the town, it had not been used. He found the team and wagon. Someone had put out fresh hay for the horses and he supposed it was Mom Lanfield. Quickly he hooked up the team, tied his own buckskin to the tailgate and drove back to the rear entrance of the Lanfield place. Mom answered his knock and led him inside again. Halfway along the corridor, Doyle put a hand on her arm, arresting her progress.

'It was a fine thing you did,' he said. 'Keeping Doris under cover this way. If the word ever got out she'd been here it would ruin her life.'

Lanfield snorted under her breath. 'Don't tell me you think I got a heart of gold or anything like that. Hell, I just don't want a weepy woman around. Makes trouble.'

'You're a liar,' Doyle said.

For a moment she was silent, and the hard old face seemed to soften. 'Once when I was a kid, if somebody had taken the time to give me a hand maybe I wouldn't be here—' She laughed harshly. 'Oh, the hell with it. Life is like a roulette wheel. Wherever the ball goes that's the slot you ride out till they finally put you in a pine box.'

'Yeah,' he said without enthusiasm. He was thinking of the Cross L and the slot he'd have to ride out for the rest of his life. Probably right into that pine box Mom Lanfield had been talking about.

'Now be careful,' Mom said. 'None of the girls knows she's been here. Don't ruin it now. You know how women talk.'

Doyle nodded. 'We'll wait till dark. It won't be long.'

In the small storeroom Doyle waited, tilted back on a packing box, smoking a cigarette. Doris was becoming rational but her terrible emotional experience had left her spent. The crazy wildness of what she had done, the possibility of humiliation for herself as well as her family, was beginning to dawn on her.

'I wanted to get back at Momma,' she said dismally. 'I wanted to be the things she accused me of being.'

'The trouble is,' Doyle interrupted, 'when we start out to hurt people, the circle gets mighty wide. Think how your dad would have felt.'

'I know.'

'And Curt.'

She looked up at the mention of Curt's name. 'Do you think Curt and I have a chance for happiness?'

'Sure you have.' He tried to put confiden in his voice, but knew it was lacking. I could you be happy with a taciturn, hateful man like Curt Barlow? But maybe the girl saw a side of him that escaped everyone else. 'You and Curt should have run away together,' Doyle said, 'instead of you coming here.'

'I know that now.' Some of the tension seemed to leave her mouth. Now she seemed small and helpless and frightened, a girl whose hatred for her stepmother had almost backfired and ruined her own life.

At dark Mom Lanfield unbolted the rear door. 'Don't worry, honey,' the old woman said. 'Nobody but us three knows you were ever here.'

Now that the enormity of her madness was upon her, Doris began to whimper. Doyle looked outside, saw no one in the thickening gloom, and led her to the wagon. Mom Lanfield gave them a brief wave of the hand and bolted the door. Through the windows they could see her moving along the corridor. Inside, the piano had started up and from uptown came the sounds of two men in a heated argument.

Doyle helped the girl to the wagon seat, then climbed in beside her and picked up the reins. Overhead the sky was clear, but the air had the clean smell of rain, which was just reaching the town. He put his slicker over Doris. He was just about to kick off the brake when he saw a heavy shadow move up to the

178

wagon on his side.

Instantly he felt a chill as he recognized Sol Dinker. 'Been watching you, Doyle,' the beefy man said. In the faint light that spilled from the windows of the Lanfield place, Doyle could see the deputy badge pinned to Dinker's shirt. 'See you take a team and wagon out of the old livery. What you up to, anyhow?'

'Nothing,' Doyle said, and put his right hand to his belt. Beside him he felt Doris trembling and knew she was hiding her head against his shoulder.

'Who you got with you, Doyle?'

'Nobody you know.'

Dinker's white teeth flashed in a grin. 'You answer or I'll take you over to the jail. Me and Joplin ain't quite sure about that Slim Dorn business.'

'He was trespassing.'

'Maybe. But it's still murder,' Dinker said. 'We might hold you in jail till we write the sheriff and see what he wants to do.'

The deputy put a big foot on the wagon step, climbed up and tried to jerk Doyle out of the way so he could see who was sitting beside him.

'Get off, Dinker,' Doyle ordered, and tried to shove him. The team was getting skittish because of the harsh voices and the threat of violence.

'Who's the girl?' Dinker deman

'Somebody special for you, or is it maybe Ellie Bar—'

Doyle's gunbarrel lifted and fell. The deputy dropped, curving backward. At the same moment the team bolted and Doyle felt the tilt off the wagon as the wheel rolled over Dinker. At the end of the alley, with mud flying from the wheels and the rain in their faces, Doyle got the team quieted and looked back. There was no movement by the rear door of Mom Lanfield's.

Grimly Doyle drove out of town.

'I've caused you real trouble now,' Doris wailed. 'When Mr. Dinker comes to, he'll arrest—' She turned in the seat, putting both hands over her mouth. 'What if the fall off the wagon killed him?' she finished feebly.

Doyle made no reply. He kept the team at a steady trot. It was nearly morning when they rode through the gate of Harvey Brome's Diamond ranch. Even though the hour was late, every window of the big house was lighted. Bitterly Doyle thought that in a week this place would be occupied by Skull Bar riders.

'Tell your dad you were staying with friends,' Doyle warned her.

'But he'll want to know who it was,' Doris said. 'Momma will especially.'

'Maybe I can fix it.'

The sound of the wagon brought Harvey me into the yard. When the rig stopped

180

Doris flung herself into his arms and after a tearful reunion the girl went into the house.

'Where'd you find her?' Harvey Brome asked anxiously.

'In town. That's all you ever need to know. And if you've got any gumption left at all, Harvey, you'll make sure that Agnes doesn't pick on the girl. Give her a chance to marry Curt Barlow, if that's what she wants.'

Brome examined his hands. 'I'm almighty grateful to you for finding her, Doyle.'

'Take Doris away from here—tomorrow. Then let her get word to Curt. If he's any kind of a man he'll follow her wherever she is.'

Brome nodded. 'All right. We'll take the stage out of Regency. Agnes kind of wants to see Denver. I'll have one of the boys here pack up my stuff and drive the wagon—' Brome clasped his hand. 'I'll see that Doris has the kind of a wedding she wants. Maybe in Denver her and Curt can find happiness.'

'I hope so,' Doyle said, but somehow couldn't believe they would ever be married. He untied his buckskin from the tailgate of the wagon and prepared to mount.

'By the way,' Brome said, 'Did you get your business fixed up with Mom Lanfield?'

Doyle kept a straight face. 'All taken care of,' he said, and Brome seemed to believe him.

Agnes came across the yard, her '

181

curlers, wearing an old wrapper. She said caustically, 'Doris won't tell where she's been. Maybe you better tell us, Mr. Doyle!'

Before Doyle could answer, Harvey Brome found his voice. 'You got to quit hounding the girl, Agnes. She'll be gone pretty soon when her and Curt is married—'

'Curt Barlow!' Agnes spat. 'I'd rather see him dead than married to Doris!'

Doyle rode out, and even after he passed through the gate he could still hear them arguing.

CHAPTER SEVENTEEN

During the night Curt Barlow lay awake, listening to the pound of the rain on the roof of the lean-to where he bunked. Usually he slept in the big house, but Jeb had been prodding to find out who had taken a whip to him. Dave knew, but his older brother had kept his mouth shut. Curt stirred in the bunk, thinking of Doris and how she had been filled with terror when her stepmother came raging from behind a shed and caught them in each other's arms. Even now Curt could feel the bite of the whiplash against his ~k.

had been a humiliating experience, and ¹ fled to his horse and ridden away, the blood soaking into the back of his shirt. Somehow he had to get Doris away from her family and marry her. Go to some new country. There was chance for a man in Idaho, he'd heard. Go there, get away from Jeb. It would be a fresh start.

But first there was a score to settle. Hamp Malgren. For two days now he had seen Malgren riding alone in the Temple Hills. He wondered at Malgren's newly-found nerve at being in Barlow country without a Skull Bar crew behind him. But he guessed now that Gunwright had secured the Brome ranch, Malgren and the rest of the hands figured they were safe no matter where they went. Riding for a powerful outfit like Skull Bar, Curt Barlow knew, gave a man a certain sense of cecurity.

Because he wanted to end this thing with Malgren personally, he had told neither Jeb nor Dave about seeing Malgren.

That morning he ate breakfast while Ellie gave him anxious looks and seemed, a time or two, on the verge of asking him who had put the marks on his back. Curt had explained his bruised mouth and cut face. 'Kermit Doyle and me tangled,' he had said, and saw Ellie go white around the mouth. He knew his sister was in love with Doyle and that to him was the greatest insult. He thoroughly hat Doyle and minded not at all letting know about it.

Without saying anything to them he got his horse, donned his slicker against the driving rain, and rode out. This morning he saw Skull Bar cows deep in the Temple Hills, far inside the boundary of Anvil. So Gunwright had the nerve to run cows on Barlow land. This plus the beating he had received at the hands of Agnes Brome, kept him in a surly and dangerous mood. It was one thing to fight a man, but because of his strict code, Curt Barlow could not lift a hand to a woman like Agnes Brome, not even to defend himself. So he had taken the beating quietly.

If anything, the rain increased, and from a promontory he watched some Skull Bar cows huddled in a ravine at the edge of the brawling Riondo Creek. By now the creek was bank to bank and if the cloudburst continued it would likely spill over and flood the lower country. That was the trouble with rain, Curt reflected sourly. It came all at once and ran off instead of soaking into the ground and raising the water level.

Although Jeb had warned them all not to venture east of Riondo Creek unless they were together, Curt meant to disobey the order. From his saddlebag he pulled an old telescope he had brought back from the war, and adjusted it on a lone figure in the ravine below. Sitting on a rock, sheltered from the rain by an overhang, was Hamp Malgren. He had his right boot off and he was rubbing his foot. Curt felt a fierce elation. Apparently the Skull Bar rider had been there for quite some time, because Curt could see his horse tied off in the thick grove that bordered one side of the canyon bottom.

This was too good a chance to miss, Malgren being alone. For a moment Curt was tempted to knock Malgren off the rock with a rifle shot. But it was quite a distance, and the first bullet might inadvertently kill him. Curt wanted the man alive. He wanted to see Jeb's face when he brought Malgren home with his hands roped behind his back.

Leaving his horse on the ridge out of sight, Curt removed his spurs and began to work his way down to the canyon floor, moving slowly so as not to slip on the wet rocks. He took advantage of every screening of brush so the man below wouldn't see him. Reaching the canyon floor, Curt eagerly drew his gun. This was so easy. He smiled and moved forward. Malgren was rubbing his foot again as if a pebble might have rubbed a blister on the bottom.

'Malgren,' Curt said.

Hamp Malgren looked up and dropped his boot. He appeared to be frightened, yet only a small degree of fear showed on his face. That puzzled Curt. Why didn't the man attempt to seize the rifle at his side? Surely he must know that the presence of a Barlow meant he was doomed to a very unpleasant death.

Something crashed in the canyon behind Curt, but even before the sound reached him, a tremendous blow against his right leg knocked him sprawling. He felt sick and numbed from shock. Instinctively he tightened the fingers of his right hand, and realized he was gripping empty air. He had dropped his revolver.

Hearing the sound of boots, he opened his eyes. Men in yellow slickers crowded around. Clyde Fengean, rain-water sparkling in his square cut beard, held a rifle, and Curt knew without being told, that it was the Skull Bar foreman who had shot him.

'Walked right into it,' Sid Gunwright said, coming up beside Fengean. He had a rain-wet smudge of mud on one smoothly shaved cheek. 'I didn't think a Barlow would be that eager,' Gunwright said. 'But he was.'

Despite the shock, Curt's mind stayed clear. He saw Malgren put on his boot and tramp up the canyon to look at him lying in the mud. 'I was scared that son was going to shoot me before you sprung the trap,' Malgren said.

Clyde Fengean grunted. 'Might not have been much loss,' the foreman said coldly.

Malgren glared at him and Gunwright said, 'That's enough, Clyde.' Then Gunwright turned, giving Malgren a thin-lidded look. 'You've got one job to do, Hamp, and you know what it is.'

'Yeah.' Malgren took a hitch at his belt.

'There's a thousand dollars in it to split with anybody you care to take in on the job.'

'Sol Dinker?' Malgren said. 'He's got a split head and he ain't forgot how he got it.'

'Handle the job your own way,' Gunwright said. 'But if you fail, don't come back.'

Malgren hesitated. Then he said, 'I'll be back, Gunwright. Don't worry about that. Just have the money ready.'

When he caught up his horse and rode off, there was a moment of uncomfortable silence. Fengean knocked a dead shell from his rifle. 'I don't blame you for risking your neck to get Malgren,' he told Curt. 'If I was in your shoes I'd feel the same way.' Then seeing the pallor on Curt's face, he asked, 'Leg hurt?'

'It hurts like hell,' Curt said.

Gunwright cut in, 'Well, don't worry. It won't bother you long.'

Fengean scrubbed the back of a hand through his wet beard. 'Still figure this is the way to do it, Sid?'

'There's no other way,' Gunwright said.

While Curt watched, a growing terror in him, two of the six Skull Bar men in the canyon roped a big steer from the brush and shot it in the head. One of the others built a small fire in a cave in the cliff wall. Still another rider had gone after Curt's horse on the bluff and now he appeared with it. The dead steer was dragged near the fire with saddle ropes. It was all neatly done, each man at his assigned task as if this had been carefully rehearsed.

Fengean gripped a two-foot length of iron rod in his hand and put it in the fire. When it was hot he worked on the brand of the dead steer. Satisfied, he straightened and put the iron back in the fire.

'Running iron, Curt,' he said to the man who lay on his back in the mud, blood pumping from a hole in his leg. He jerked a thumb at the dead steer. 'You did a clumsy job on that Skull Bar brand.'

Curt's mouth went dry, and his pain fled before the awful certainty of his doom.

If there had been any doubt as to the outcome, it was eternally settled when Fengean turned to a fat man with a sickly pallor on his face. 'Get me a rope, O'Shane.'

Tim O'Shane got the rope, but was trembling so he could not hold it. The coil slipped from his hands, and with a laugh, Fengean picked it up. They carried Curt up the canyon to a giant cottonwood, its crown blackened from lightning, but its lower limbs stout. Despite the rain Curt could see the ground kicked up where he and Kermit Doyle had fought. And there was the deadfall where Curt had sat with Doris Brome.

The rope was flung over a limb. The leaves sparkled, washed clean of dust by the rain.

On the trunk were the initials he had carved last year when he and Doris first started going around together. He found them with his eyes, the carving no longer fresh and clean but darkened from the weather. It was the last thing he saw before they hanged him.

*　　　*　　　*

Never in her life had Sabrina Hale known such terror. She wanted to scream, and when the agony of it was hard in her throat, she fought desperately against it. Soaked by the rain, she huddled behind a rock, watching the men in the canyon below. She had been on the upper trail, riding for Doyle's Cross L, when she saw the Skull Bar men below her.

Last night in town she had learned how Doyle and three former Skull Bar men had retaken the Cross L. Sid Gunwright had told her, but seemed willing to forget the matter for the present, which surprised her. Perhaps his easy acquisition of the Brome ranch made him confident of eventually taking over the entire hill country without too much trouble. She only knew that last night Gunwright had seemed unusually reserved with her, casually polite, and this made her frightened and unsure of herself. He had some business that would take him to Prescott for a week, he had told her last night. He was taking the early stage this morning, he said. When she heard that, Sabrina put on a black riding habit and, in mid-morning, started north. With Kermit Doyle in possession of the Cross L, even though only temporarily, it would give her a chance to destroy the contents of her trunk before Sid returned from Prescott.

She remembered with a chill what he had told her last night. 'Your friend Doyle must have been living with a woman at Cross L. Some of my men found a trunk full of clothes. I'll ride out and take a look at them when I come back from Prescott. After I kick Doyle out, of course.'

She had stood looking at him, unable to find her voice.

'By the way, whatever happened to that pink dress I liked so much? I haven't seen you wear it for months—six months, at least.' Then he had left her, ostensibly to buy his ticket on the stage.

With Gunwright out of town, her only fear was that one of the Skull Bar men might see her heading for Doyle's place. But it was a calculated risk.

At first, when she saw them in the canyon, she was surprised that Gunwright, instead of going to Prescott as he had said, was now standing with Clyde Fengean, looking at someone on the ground. From where she hid it looked like Curt Barlow, but she couldn't be sure until they jerked him to his feet. They carried him up the canyon, then tied his hands and put him on a horse. It was Fengean who rode close and put the noose over Curt Barlow's head and tightened it.

Sid Gunwright, standing beside Barlow's horse, an unlighted cigar in his teeth, removed his hat and struck the rump of Barlow's horse with it. The horse bolted and went racing up the canyon. Nobody bothered to go after it. Sid Gunwright's voice was clear and she heard him say, 'Give me a match, Clyde. I've used mine up.' Gunwright stepped around the swaying, jerking thing at the end of the rope, so Fengean could hand him down a match. Shielding the flame from the rain, Gunwright lighted his cigar, then said, 'Let's get out of here.'

CHAPTER EIGHTEEN

After the long ride from Regency to the Brome ranch with Doris, and thence to the Cross L, Doyle was weary of the saddle. He sat on the veranda of his house, watching the rain boil up the surface of Riondo Creek, and pondered the sudden appearance of Sol Dinker outside the rear door of the Lanfield place. Had Dinker been playing a game, trying to make Doyle reveal Doris Brome's identity or didn't he really know? One thing for sure, Doyle told himself: it would be unsafe for him to be seen alone in Regency. Dinker had hated him enough before he'd knocked the deputy off the Brome wagon. Now Dinker would be murderous.

The sound of a horse in the canyon caused Doyle to pitch his cigarette over the porch rail. As it died against the wet ground with a wisp of blue smoke, he jerked up the rifle he had placed under his chair and peered through the wet leaves of the aspens.

Pete Tasker, who was cooking the evening meal, also had heard the horse. He came to the door, tall and red-headed, wearing his gun. At the kitchen table, Prince and Al Miller looked up from their stud game.

Doyle felt an immense relief when he saw Ellie Barlow ride through the trees. The girl lifted a hand in greeting and managed a smile. The old slicker she wore over her trim figure had ripped at the shoulders and front.

'I'll take your horse, ma'am,' Pete Tasker said when Ellie slipped to the ground. Then he yelled at the two men inside, saying they ought to scout around and see if any Skull Bar men might be lurking in the shadows. Doyle smiled his thanks for this courtesy of leaving him alone with the girl.

Ellie sank to a bench on the porch. Shadows were deep along the western edge of the canyon. Riondo Creek roared over its banks and Doyle knew that if the rain didn't let up they could be flooded out.

'You shouldn't ride alone,' Doyle told Ellie. 'Not with Malgren still loose.'

Her blue eyes were serious. 'I'll never be caught out again without a gun,' she said, and touched a small revolver shoved into her belt. Then she leaned forward, clasping her hands. 'I've talked to Dad and Dave,' she said. 'I've finally convinced them that without unity we have no chance for survival. It will only be a matter of time until Gunwright moves in, and either kills off the Barlows on some pretext or other or makes them a ridiculous offer for their land that they'll be forced to accept.'

'What does Curt think about it?' Doyle said, thinking that if anyone would wreck these plans of Ellie's it would be her dark and taciturn brother.

'Curt will do whatever Dad says,' Ellie said. 'He was gone when we had our talk, but when he comes back tonight Dad will tell him.'

Doyle still was not convinced. 'The Temple Hills Pool died at birth,' he said. 'Brome sold out to Gunwright.'

Then he noticed, through the front of her torn slicker, that her shirt was soaked from the rain and clung to her full breasts. He drew her into the house where the warmth from the stove soon put color back in her cheeks. He called Pete Tasker. The Texan helped him move Sabrina's trunk in from the shed, then went outside again.

Doyle felt a foreboding, for the ropes that had held the trunk had been cut and he knew someone had opened it. But he philosophically shrugged it off. The damage was done now. But when he lifted the lid and watched the pure pleasure in Ellie's animated face, he had to smile. Gently her hands touched the fine fabrics, drawing out dress after dress, exclaiming over each one.

'Take your pick and put it on,' he said.

'The pink one,' she said, pleased. In her excitement she did not question him as to the ownership of the clothes. Perhaps she guessed, he told himself, but had been so long without any garments to match these (or perhaps never had had them) that she seemed oblivious to all else.

'When your own clothes are dry,' he said, 'I'll give you a good slicker and ride you home.'

'All right,' she said, her eyes bright. Then she saw him frown at something beyond the window. 'What's the matter, Kermit?'

'The creek is rising,' he said, and knew a cloudburst higher in the mountains had sent down a wall of water over three feet high. Now the creek had spread across half the canyon floor and he knew it might be several hours before they could cross it and thus reach the Barlow ranch.

He turned, but Ellie apparently had considered this news of no great moment. She had gone into the bedroom. Hesitating a moment, he finally knocked on the door. She ought to know about the creek, he told himself. She opened the door, holding the shirt she had removed over her breasts. Seeing her this way, with her gleaming shoulders, he forgot what he had come to tell her. For a quarter of a minute they stood looking at each other, and gradually a flush spread across her cheeks. She moistened her lips.

Then she gave him a wan smile. 'It was quite an idea of Dad's to have you marry me,' she murmured. 'But it would be no good without love, would it, Kermit?'

He took a step toward her, but she gently put a hand against his chest, pushed him from the room and closed the door. He felt oddly excited when he went outside to pump a coffee pot full of water. The rain had tapered off to a drizzle and he knew that already the storm had passed, bringing a slight respite from the drought on the Flats.

He turned back into the house, dumped coffee into the pot and then went to the back door. He could see the three Texans standing under the shed eaves out of the rain, smoking and talking. He was about to tell them to come in the house out of the cold when he heard a commotion in the yard.

Flinging open the front door, he saw that Sabrina Hale had ridden a blown horse into the yard. She swayed in the saddle, her hair wet and loose about her pale face.

'Kermit!' she cried, and would have fallen into the mud had not Tasker sprinted from the shed and caught her in his arms.

Charlie Prince caught her horse when it started to wheel toward the aspen grove. Doyle held the door open while Pete Tasker carried Sabrina into the house and laid her on a couch. As he saw her lying tense, biting her lips, her eyes tightly closed, he knew she had experienced some shock. He tried to imagine what urgency had caused her to ride out here in the storm. And how could she have crossed the rising creek? But then he knew she had probably come out from Regency where the road was on the east side of the creek all the way.

'What you reckon ails her?' Pete Tasker said gravely, and Doyle could not help but remember that the Texan had more than once expressed his love for this pale and shaken woman who was beginning to utter a low, moaning sound.

Because he did not know what she might say when she awoke, Doyle jerked his head at Tasker, urging him to go outside where Miller and Prince were standing uncertainly on the porch.

'I never in my whole life figured I'd get this close to Sabrina Hale,' Tasker said. He seemed awed. At the door he turned and

196

looked back at her. Then he went out to the porch and closed the door behind him. The three of them peered through the window at Sabrina.

Doyle had heard the bedroom door open behind him. Now he turned, seeing Ellie wearing the pink dress. She had pinned up her hair and in the dress she looked grown up and really more beautiful than Sabrina. Of that he was sure. There was not the hardness around the mouth, nor the calculating eye of Sabrina.

He placed a finger on his lips and said, 'Leave me alone with her a minute.'

Ellie looked at him gravely, then stepped back into the bedroom and closed the door.

Barely had Ellie left the room than Sabrina seemed to force her eyes open. She peered up from the couch as if not recognizing Doyle for a moment. Then she gave a little cry of anguish and caught his wrists and drew him close. He knelt on one knee beside the couch, suddenly feeling sorry for her.

'Tell me, Sabrina. What's the matter?'

'Kermit—Kermit—' She closed her eyes.

Hoping he could start her talking he said, 'You're unnerved. The storm frightened you.' He bent closer, his face grim. 'It was the storm, wasn't it?'

When she opened her hazel eyes he saw a stark terror in their depths. 'Oh, Kermit,' she moaned, and clutched his hand. 'It was awful. Horrible.' She closed her eyes again, as if to shut out the terrible memory of whatever it was she had witnessed. 'And Sid stood there smugly and struck the horse with his hat. Then he asked Fengean for a match.' She shuddered.

'What are you talking about, Sabrina?'

'The other night I said that I was without conscience, that I was hard.' She gave a shrill laugh, then bit her lip. Beneath the line of her dark hair he could see tiny beads of moisture. 'I said I was like Sid Gunwright. But I'm not, Kermit.'

'Tell me what happened?' he said sharply.

She flung an arm across her eyes. 'I want you to take me away from this country, Kermit. We could live in Denver. Money isn't so important to me now.'

'You know that's over and done, Sabrina.'

She looked at him and there was hate in her eyes. 'Then if you'd turn from me there must be another woman in your life.'

But he forced the conversation back on her. 'What happened to change your mind about Gunwright?'

'He's a cold-hearted killer.' The memory was back in her again and he saw a shudder rack her slender body.

Doyle felt the roof of his mouth go dry, knowing she had seen some horror this day that had completely stunned her. And he dreaded to know what it was, yet he knew he must. 'You'd better tell me why you regard Gunwright as a killer all of a sudden.'

'He hanged Curt Barlow.'

Doyle rose. At the same moment the bedroom door crashed open. Ellie Barlow rushed across the room, the hem of the full pink dress whirling about her white legs. She came to stand at the edge of the couch and peer down at Sabrina. 'You're a liar!' she cried. There was mingled in her voice a fury and a dread of the truth. 'They couldn't hang my brother!'

Doyle caught her by the shoulders, but Ellie squirmed out of his grasp. Behind him he heard Sabrina's squeal of rage, her quick indrawn breath, and knew what it meant. Yet even in that tense moment he realized it was the first time since the trial that he had seen Ellie Barlow dressed up. Her hair was pinned up and there were tiny ringlets of coppery hair around her ears. Evidently she had found high-heeled slippers in the trunk and they made her look taller and fully as elegant as Sabrina Hale at her best. All this Doyle saw in the instant the two women glared at each other. There was anger and fear on Ellie's face, quick hatred in Sabrina's.

Sabrina managed to sit up. Her face was even whiter than before and despite witnessing death this day, she seemed even more furious at seeing Ellie Barlow here. 'She's wearing *my* dress!' Sabrina cried. 'My dress!' Suddenly she leaped to her feet and lunged at the girl. Doyle caught her around the waist and flung her back on the couch.

'There's no need for that,' he said.

But Sabrina rose, her mouth twisted bitterly. She began to laugh and cry at the same time. 'You've been living here with Ellie Barlow!' Her voice rose to a hysterical pitch. 'And you gave her my clothes to wear.' Despite the moral aspect of the thing, Sabrina seemed to find the fact that the Barlow girl was attired in her dress the greater insult.

'Shut up, Sabrina!' Doyle said, and attempted to push her back to the couch again. She extended her hands and tried to claw him in the face. He stepped back, sick and disgusted. All this show of temper over a few clothes when Curt Barlow had been lynched . . .

Sabrina hunched over, damp hair loose about her face, black riding habit as mud-stained as her boots.

Ellie stood stiffly, head thrown back, the fear in her growing. 'Did you really see them hang my brother—'

But Sabrina seemed possessed of but a single thought. 'My clothes!' she screamed again, whirling on Doyle. 'Hamp Malgren was right! He found you and Ellie together. And you tried to kill him—'

Again she tried to reach Ellie and claw her face. Ellie stood her ground, and just as

Sabrina was about to crowd the younger girl across the room in her fury, Doyle struck her across the face. The suddenness of the blow dropped Sabrina to her knees. She huddled on the floor, weeping quietly.

Feeling a blast of cold air on the back of his neck, Doyle turned. He saw Pete Tasker. The Texan had been watching through the window. His face was black with rage.

For a moment the two men regarded each other and Doyle sensed that Tasker was only a breath away from dragging out his gun. Doyle said, 'Don't be a fool, Pete.'

'I don't hold with hitting a woman,' the big Texan snarled.

'Please,' Ellie begged. 'Hasn't there been enough trouble?'

But at that moment Sabrina rose to her feet, trembling. She looked ghastly and across one cheek were the red marks left by Doyle's open hand. 'I hate you, Kermit,' she said, her voice acid. 'How I hate you!'

Suddenly, before Doyle could stop her, she ran from the house. He heard her horse plunging across the muddy yard.

'Go after her, Pete,' Doyle said. 'See that she gets back to town.'

The red-haired Texan gave Doyle a level look. 'I'll do that. And I won't be back.' From the door he added, 'And I reckon that'll go for Al and Charlie when I tell 'em!'

He lunged through the doorway. The

there were the hoofbeats of three horses galloping down the canyon road after Sabrina. When silence had again spread through the house Doyle felt a raw sickness in the pit of his stomach. Ellie stood facing the blank wall, her face drained of all color.

'She was lying,' Ellie said in a strange numbed voice. 'Gunwright didn't hang Curt.'

Wishing to ease her burden, Doyle said, 'Sabrina was hysterical. She might have thought she saw something she didn't see at all. The eyes sometimes play tricks on a person.'

'You don't really believe that,' Ellie said.

He made no reply.

'I'm going to find out for sure,' Ellie said. She picked up her wet clothing from the chair where they had been drying in front of the stove. Doyle got out an old wool shirt of his which he gave her. She took it without comment and disappeared into the bedroom.

Doyle sank to the edge of the couch and stared at the floor. He could hear the sound of water dripping from the eaves and in the distance, the roar of Riondo Creek.

CHAPTER NINETEEN

Although Ellie and Doyle searched the canyon until midnight, they found no trace of

Curt. It was possible, Doyle reasoned, that the Skull Bar had caught him in some place that was now inaccessible because of the cloudburst. There were Skull Bar cows in these hills now and that meant Skull Bar riders. It was increasingly dangerous, but this grim business had taken such a turn that Doyle was no longer concerned for his own safety.

Back at Cross L he pulled Ellie from the saddle, and she came against him. They stood together a moment, neither speaking in the dark and silent yard.

'I'll stay here tonight,' she said. 'By morning the creek should be down, and we can get across and look for Curt.'

She went into the house and as he put up the horses he could hear the roar of Riondo Creek, which had become a raging river, fed by the cloudbursts from the higher peaks. Later, he gave Ellie the bedroom and rolled up on the couch in a blanket.

Shortly before dawn he heard the sound of horses in the yard. Snatching up his gun, he crept to a window.

'Doyle!' a man called, and he recognized Dave Barlow's voice.

After lighting a lantern, Doyle drew his revolver and stepped to the porch. He saw that Jeb Barlow had swung down and now stood with head bowed. The old man seemed to have shrunk in stature and he kept a ha-

pressed against his chest.

Tall and grim, his mustache speckled with mud from the trail, Dave Barlow stepped up. 'Curt's horse come home. We backtracked it in the mud.' He took a deep breath. 'We found Curt and me and Pa cut him down.'

Jeb Barlow lifted his head. He looked old and sick and still kept the hand tight against his chest as if to pressure away a pain. 'The creek rose up after we crossed,' he said, 'and we can't get back. I'd like Curt to have a warm place for the rest of the night—'

'Bring him in,' Doyle said, then added grimly, 'Ellie's here.'

Either Jeb did not comprehend or he was too crushed by the death of his son to care. He said nothing as he shuffled into the house.

Dave said, 'Ellie told us she was going to ride over here.' He cut Curt loose from the horse and carried him into the house and laid him on the couch. Doyle looked down, feeling sick. Doris would have a long wait for her Curt. The rest of her life. The noose had strangled him, and the falling of his body had broken sinew and bone.

Ellie came into the room, picked up Doyle's blanket from where it had dropped on the floor, and covered Curt with it.

Doyle saw that she had dressed in her denim pants and his wool shirt. She gazed down at the blanket-covered object on the couch. But there were no tears. Only her

204

lower lip trembled. Doyle stepped to her side and put an arm about her.

'She slept in the bedroom,' he said, for Jeb was looking at them. 'I slept out here.'

Jeb sank to a chair. 'Don't matter. Nothin' matters. Curt's dead. He went through the war. He never got touched. Then he comes home and they hang him.' He stared at the floor, tracked by muddy boots. 'You got any whisky, Doyle?'

Doyle found a bottle the Skull Bar outfit had left behind. He filled glasses and they drank to Curt Barlow. And either the bite of the liquor or her grief brought tears to Ellie's eyes. She went into the bedroom and closed the door.

The men drank steadily, but none of them felt the whisky, Doyle least of all. Gradually the numbness that had gripped him turned to rage. He had never liked the arrogant, mean-tempered, Curt. But Curt was a human being, and the Skull Bar had killed him.

Doyle told them how Sabrina had witnessed Curt's death. And Dave said that when they found Curt there was a dead Skull Bar cow beside a branding fire. The cow's Skull Bar brand had been worked into a Barlow Anvil with a running iron.

'Gunwright scared out Harvey Brome without firing a shot,' Doyle said. 'I wonder how many of them will quit when they hear about Curt.'

Jeb Barlow said dully, 'We got to bury Curt.'

'Rifle Pass is close,' Doyle suggested. 'You can see it for miles. Every time you look up there you'll know that's where Curt is buried.'

Jeb nodded, seemingly pleased at Doyle's suggestion. 'But we got no flag,' the old man said, as if this fact were of supreme importance. 'He ought to be buried in Jeff Davis's flag.' He lifted his head. 'See if the creek is down, Dave. We got to get that flag.'

From the window Dave said, 'It ain't down, Pa. We can't get home for a spell.'

Old Jeb seemed crushed.

Doyle stepped to the shed and rummaged through his portmanteau. From the small trunk he drew a large package wrapped in newspapers. This he carried back into the house and laid it on the table. The Barlows crowded around, for they seemed to sense that something of importance was about to be revealed.

'I don't have a flag,' Doyle said, 'but maybe this will do.'

He broke the strings and unwrapped the package. Jeb Barlow stared, his eyes wide. 'You wore the gray,' he murmured, peering at Doyle as if seeing a stranger. His voice rose. 'You was on our side. A captain, by hell.' Some of his grief at Curt's passing gave way to amazement as he fingered the soiled,

206

worn uniform.

Dave Barlow seemed utterly stunned. 'Why didn't you never tell us, Doyle?' he demanded.

'The war is over,' Doyle said. 'I wanted to forget it.'

Ellie's lips were white as she looked at her father and brother. 'You were willing enough to kill him,' she said sharply, 'when you thought he was a Yankee.'

Jeb Barlow's eyes blazed and he stepped to Doyle's side and placed a gnarled hand on the younger man's shoulder. 'We'll fight together like we done in the war, Doyle. We'll whip Gunwright—'

His fervor had carried him away and he winced with pain and gripped his chest with both hands. Dave sprang forward and lowered the old man to a chair. 'Take it a little easy, Pa. You dyin' here from that bad heart won't help us lick Skull Bar.'

Jeb Barlow tried a crooked grin. His face was gray, and he took a drink from the whisky bottle on the table, despite Ellie's protests.

'Soon's I get my breath,' Jeb said, 'we'll ride.'

*   *   *

Lew Gorling sat on a box in the Skull Bar yard, his left arm in a sling. He was enjoying the sun that was drying out the yard after the rain. Even now in some places there was little evidence of the cloudburst. He saw horsemen break over the horizon, and yelled at Skip Harlow. The old cook came to the cookshack door and peered out.

'It's all right,' he told the yellow-haired rider. 'They're Skull Bar.' Together they watched a dozen men move slowly into the yard. They were mud-splattered and their faces showed the weariness that comes from long hours in the saddle. Gorling gave a start when he saw that two of the riders were Al Miller and Charlie Prince. Their arms were bound to their sides, their ankles lashed to stirrups.

Hamp Malgren seemed in charge. The big black-haired rider seemed surly and impatient when Gorling asked what happened and where was Pete Tasker.

'Got away,' Malgren said shortly. 'Tasker and these two—' he jerked a thumb at the tight-lipped prisoners—'were ridin' with the Hale woman. We just happened to jump them on the way back to Regency. Tasker and the woman got away, but we boxed these boys.' He gave the two Texans a hard look, remembering the night they had turned against him in favor of Doyle. 'If I had my way I'd kill 'em now. But Gunwright wants to wait till he gets Conodine over from the county seat. Then if everything goes all right, we'll bury these two out here somewheres.'

'Where's Gunwright now?' Gorling wanted to know.

'In Regency,' Malgren said. 'And that's where I'm headin' myself. There's big things in the wind, boys. It's the showdown at last.' He saw that the two prisoners, still tied, were left in the tool shed under guard. 'You let them two get away,' he warned the men he was leaving behind, 'and you'll get worse'n Curt Barlow.'

CHAPTER TWENTY

Dressed in the uniform of Captain Kermit Doyle, late of Shelby's command, Curt Barlow was buried in the wind-swept and lonely Rifle Pass. None of them had a Bible, but Jeb Barlow mumbled a passage of Scripture he remembered from his boyhood in the Missouri hills.

When it was over and Doyle and Dave Barlow had covered the grave, old Jeb said, 'When I'm gone I want to be buried here. Beside Curt.'

'All right, Pa,' Dave said.

Jeb put a hand to his chest. 'When we settle this fight,' the old man vowed, 'I'll put up a tombstone here for Curt.' His mouth twisted in pain, and he turned for his horse.

'Let's get on with the fightin',' he finished.

Later, descending the steep road from the pass, they suddenly came upon four riders who had just made a bend in the canyon. Tom Joplin and Sol Dinker, deputy badges prominent on their shirt fronts, showed their surprise. With them were Hamp Malgren and his cousin, Anse Lipscomb. The men sat their saddles stiffly. Dinker's face bore a wicked gash and one eye was purple.

Hamp Malgren found his voice. 'We been hunting you,' he said and hesitated, not wishing to be the first to draw a gun and, therefore, perhaps the first to die.

Cursing, Jeb moved his horse from Dave's mount and Doyle was afraid the old man might do something reckless that would endanger the girl's life.

Doyle said quietly, 'Let Ellie get away, Hamp. Then we'll settle this thing with you.'

But it was the lanky, tobacco-chewing Tom Joplin who said, 'Ain't nothing to settle. You're all under arrest.' His mean eyes shifted to Doyle. 'This time you won't stay so long in our jail. You and the Barlows will hang, and the gal will likely get life at Yuma, which maybe is worse.'

Doyle felt perspiration break out under his armpits as he sat his horse there in the narrow canyon. Ahead, in the distance, he could see a wisp of smoke that marked the site of Regency. Already the road was drying out.

Before another day's sun was on it, the dust would coil upward again around whoever passed this way.

'Are we accused of something?' Doyle demanded, edging his horse around, 'or are you just making this up as you go along?'

'You murdered Al Miller and Charlie Prince last night,' Hamp Malgren said tensely. 'Shot 'em right out of their saddles. You don't kill Skull Bar men without paying for it.'

Doyle was shocked. But were the two Texans really dead, or was this another of Gunwright's elaborate fabrications?

'You forgot one thing,' Doyle said, trying to prolong this stalemate as long as possible. He tried to catch Ellie's eyes, but the girl sat rigid in her saddle, her face white. 'Prince and Miller weren't riding for Skull Bar. They quit.'

'Your word,' Sol Dinker said. His eyes were murderous and he seemed anxious to get this thing started.

'Bluff won't do no good,' Malgren said.

Doyle's right hand was tense above the butt of his revolver. In him was a measure of grief for the pair who had followed Pete Tasker from the Cross L last night. Malgren had made no mention of Sabrina or Tasker, and Doyle wondered if they had got safely to town.

'Fengean and Gunwright seen you do the

211

shooting,' Sol Dinker said suddenly, and started a hand for his gun.

Doyle jerked a foot from a stirrup, booted Ellie's horse on the flank and drew his revolver.

The Barlows were driven apart as Ellie's horse went crashing into the wet brush that grew thick against the base of the cliff. And Tom Joplin barely kept his own saddle as his horse, spooked by the plunging Barlow mounts, reared and nearly went over backwards. In that moment Doyle fired at Hamp Malgren. But he missed when the man drove in the spurs and got away from Dave Barlow who was bearing down on him.

Doyle veered his buckskin and saw Dinker shooting at Jeb Barlow. He sent his horse head on into the fat deputy's mount. As Dinker tried to swing around for another try at Jeb, Doyle, unable to get a clean shot, brought down the barrel of his gun with a sickening smash across the crown of the deputy's hat. Without a sound Dinker dropped loosely to the ground, his hat rolling under the hoofs of Doyle's horse. The deputy's skull was split as if by an ax.

A gun roared almost in Doyle's ear and he felt the burn of powder along his neck. In the press of horses and shouting men, Doyle's pivoting buckskin rammed Malgren's roan. Knocked off balance, the buckskin started to go down. Doyle leaped and flung his arms about Malgren's neck, and the two of them fell heavily to the muddy ground. Doyle rose quickly.

Knowing he was lucky to retain a grip on his gun, Doyle stood spraddle-legged over Malgren and pointed the weapon at him. But Malgren did not move. He lay on his back, slack-jawed and unconscious.

No longer hearing gun fire, Doyle looked around. Jeb and Dave Barlow had crowded Joplin against a cliff, and the lank deputy had lifted his hands. Joplin was staring at his partner who lay on the wet ground, the harsh sunlight revealing a bluish gray substance in the crack in his skull. Both Joplin and Anse Lipscomb, the latter sitting loose in his saddle, big face pale, seemed a little ill at the sight of Dinker.

Ellie had got her frightened horse under control, and now sat behind Lipscomb, the muzzle of her rifle pointed at the stableman's back.

Joplin licked his lips and forgot his sickness long enough to say shakily, 'You've killed a deputy sheriff, Doyle.' A worm of brown tobacco juice angled across his bony chin. 'When Conodine hears about this, he'll get you if it takes ten years.'

Jeb Barlow grinned at him. 'Now just who do you reckon is goin' to tell the sheriff?'

'I am,' Joplin snapped. And then he went pale around the mouth as old Jeb, still

213

grinning, thumb-twiddled the hammer of the Bisley revolver he held in his steady hand. 'You wouldn't shoot me and Anse in cold blood—' Joplin's voice trailed off. He looked sick again, but for a different reason.

Doyle eyed Joplin, remembering the misery this deputy had caused him in jail. 'Why wouldn't we murder you?' he demanded. 'We're the type. You've already told us we killed Al Miller and Charlie Prince.'

Joplin started to speak, then bogged down.

Doyle's gaze hardened. 'Who really killed Prince and Miller?'

'I only know what Gunwright told me,' the deputy hedged.

'And what about Pete Tasker and Sabrina? Did they get away?'

It was Anse Lipscomb, big and awkward in the saddle, who suddenly blurted, 'Sabrina's in town. I seen her.'

Doyle studied the pair, wishing he had the nerve to finish the job and be done with it. But murder, even though it might seem necessary, was not in his code. 'You give this message to Gunwright. The next Skull Bar man we find in Temple Hills we'll hang.' Then he turned to Dave and Jeb. 'Let them go.'

Jeb argued, but Doyle was adamant. Joplin and Anse Lipscomb were not Skull Bar, he said, even though they might be drawing

214

money from Gunwright. But Hamp Malgren
... Malgren was different.

Relieved of their guns and still shaken by
their narrow squeak from death, Lipscomb
and Joplin spurred down the canyon without
a backward glance at Malgren.

The black-haired Skull Bar man stirred, sat
up and looked around. He saw Dinker's body
and the ugly wound on the deputy's head.
Slowly Malgren got to his feet. From her
saddle Ellie stared at him coldly, no sign on
her beautiful face that she had ever seen this
man before.

Doyle walked over and handed up his
revolver to her, butt foremost. 'Do you want
to do it, Ellie? I think you're entitled to shoot
him for what he tried to do to you.'

Malgren's mouth hung open as he stared at
the girl. 'Listen. I was drunk that day. Didn't
know what I was doin'—'

Ignoring the gun Doyle held up to her,
Ellie turned her horse and rode slowly down
the canyon, and when Doyle jerked his head
at Jeb and his son, they followed her.

'This is between you and me, Hamp,'
Doyle said softly. And while Malgren looked
on, sick-eyed, Doyle crossed the road and
picked up the rider's fallen gun. Still gripping
his own revolver, and keeping his eyes on
Malgren so he didn't panic and try to get
away, Doyle knocked mud from Malgren's
gun. Then he placed the weapon on a

flat-topped rock at the edge of the road. Doyle stepped back twenty paces or so and placed his own gun on the road. Then he backed up until both he and Malgren were an equal distance from their weapons.

Sweat began to pour down Malgren's forehead. 'What you aiming to do?' he cried hoarsely.

'You were going to give me a chance that night out of Regency,' Doyle reminded him. 'I'm handing it right back to you. I'm counting to five. If you don't pick up your gun by that time, I'll get mine and kill you with it.'

Malgren spread his hands. His face seemed to collapse and with it went his viciousness. All that remained was a frightened shell of a man.

'Wait, Doyle. I can tell you things you'll want to know about Gunwright! He hanged Curt Barlow—'

Doyle began to count: 'One—two—three—'

Malgren's knees buckled a little. Then, gripped by sheer desperation, he straightened. He plunged forward, striking the ground on his chest. Snatching up his gun from the rock, he thumbed back the hammer and fired. But in his frenzy the bullet merely chipped loose some sandstone high up on the cliff wall behind Doyle. He never got a second chance. Doyle shot him in the face. It

216

was the only time in his life he ever killed a man without regret.

They buried Malgren and Sol Dinker, and then, because Harvey Brome's ranch was not too far away, Doyle said he wanted to stop by the place. Jeb and Dave did not guess his reasons, but Ellie, with a woman's intuition, had divined her brother's love for Doris Brome.

Later, at the Brome gate, he asked Ellie and the Barlow father and son to stay behind. He saw a loaded wagon in the yard, and beyond, a freighter piled high with household furnishings. Brome and the wife and children were about to take the small wagon and drive to Regency for the stage.

Doyle called Brome aside, and Agnes, her gaze sharp, trailed along. 'How's Doris?' Doyle asked.

'Still sulky,' Agnes cut in before her husband could reply. 'Sittin' in the house.'

'In a new country maybe Doris will have a chance to forget what's happened here. Maybe a few scars will be healed.'

Agnes Brome said, 'She's got nothing to regret here.'

'Now, Agnes,' Brome said, and there was a new firmness in his tone. He looked at Doyle, perhaps sensing the reason for his being here. 'Has something happened to Curt?'

'Yeah?'

'Agnes said, 'Maybe some other girl's
217

mother took a horsewhip to him.'

'You won't ever have to worry about Curt and Doris again,' Doyle said crisply. 'He's dead.'

Both Harvey Brome and his wife stood rigid. After a moment Agnes said, 'But why? How?' She seemed stunned.

'He was hanged. It was Skull Bar.' Doyle looked hard at Agnes. 'If you've got any humanity in you at all you'll get the girl out of here—now. And see that she never hears of what happened to Curt!'

Agnes Brome raised a trembling hand to her forehead. 'Oh, God,' she murmured. 'Why couldn't I have let her and Curt alone.'

'That's the trouble with regrets,' Doyle said, and turned his horse. 'They're always a little late.'

CHAPTER TWENTY-ONE

Word of Curt Barlow's death spread through the hills with lightning rapidity. When Doyle and the Barlows returned to the Cross L they found some of the members of the defunct Temple Hills Pool waiting for them: the Dunkle brothers, Bert Smalling and Lew Harper. They were carrying rifles and the apprehension left their faces when they saw it was Doyle who rode up. They had been expecting Gunwright's Skull Bar outfit to appear.

The men crowded around Jeb and Dave and offered condolences. In the manner of their kind the two Barlows accepted them gruffly. The men acted as if they personally had a hand in Curt's death.

'If Harvey Brome hadn't sold out to Gunwright,' the peppery Bert Smalling said, 'the pool wouldn't have caved in on us. Maybe Curt would be alive—'

Jeb whirled on him, his face livid. 'Talk won't bring back the dead!' he cried. He extended a heavy revolver in his gnarled hand. 'But this gun will sure help ease the feelings of them that's left behind!'

The rattle of a wagon caused them to turn to the road. Doyle saw Loren Pellman driving across Riondo Creek, which by this time had nearly returned to its original banks. Doyle knew that Pellman risked life and his future in the community to drive out here. The plump saloonman was perspiring and Doyle gave him a drink from a canteen. Ellie had gone into the house to cook a meal for the men and now she peered out the door to see who had come. She waved at Pellman.

Pellman drew Doyle aside. 'Sheriff Conodine has arrived in Regency,' Pellman said. 'He's organizing a posse to hunt you and the Barlows.'

'We didn't kill Charlie Prince and Al

Miller,' Doyle said grimly.

'I don't believe you did either. But Conodine has Gunwright's sworn statement that he and Fengean saw you shoot down two Skull Bar men.'

Doyle stood with his back to an aspen, smoking a cigarette and considering the grim news. 'Prince and Miller had already quit the Gunwright outfit,' he said.

'Maybe so,' Pellman agreed. 'But Conodine don't know that.'

'Gunwright saw a chance to pin murder on us so he shot Al and Charlie,' Doyle said. Then he added, 'I suppose Conodine has seen their bodies.'

Pellman rubbed his fat jaw. 'That's the funny part of it, Kermit. Gunwright claims when the two men was shot they fell into Sunrise Gorge.'

Doyle frowned. Sunrise Gorge was a ravine nearly a mile deep and almost inaccessible. If the two bodies were really there it would be almost impossible to get down and bring them out. A faint hope stirred in him. What if Gunwright had run the two Texans out of the country or taken them prisoner? It seemed just a little too pat for the men to have fallen into a place like Sunrise Gorge, so deep that the Utes living west of the Flats had thought the sun rose out of it each morning.

But there was the business of Sol Dinker. The deputy was dead, buried near Rifle Pass.

Even if Conodine happened to dislike his deputy personally, he would have to exert the full pressure of his office to remove the stain of the killing from the law badge Dinker had carried.

Doyle finished his cigarette. At the far end of the yard the Dunkle brothers and the other small ranchers were talking to the Barlows. Occasionally they shot an anxious glance toward Doyle and the saloonman.

'What about Sabrina?' Doyle asked.

'She keeps to her house, day and night.'

'Do you know Pete Tasker when you see him?'

Pellman nodded. 'He's either quit the country or he's holed up somewheres.'

Doyle frowned, having an idea where Tasker might be hiding. 'Will you take Ellie Barlow back to town with you?' Doyle asked him.

'Sure, if she'll ride with me.'

Doyle went into the house. He caught Ellie at the stove, turned her around and looked down into her face.

'Malgren's dead, so you don't have to worry about him,' he told her. 'I'd like you to stay at the Regency Hotel till this is over.'

She shook her head. 'My place is here.'

'But you've got to realize, Ellie—' He groped for words that would convince this girl she belonged in the comparative safety of town. 'We've got a job to do here. If you stay,

221

I'll spend all my time worrying about you instead of concentrating on the job.'

She gave him a faint smile. 'Would you worry about me, Kermit?'

For answer he hugged her to him. Her arms went tight about his neck and her mouth found his. Then she drew back and gazed at him with her serious eyes.

'Promise me this,' she said. 'If everything goes to pieces here, you'll get word to me to meet you some place.' She sighed. 'Life wouldn't be very much without you.'

'I promise,' he said, and kissed her again.

He helped her finish the meal she had been cooking on the stove. After everyone had eaten, Doyle rode with the Pellman wagon as far as the edge of the Flats. Ellie turned and waved back. For half an hour he watched the progress of the wagon across the basin, knowing that Gunwright would not be fool enough to attack Pellman and the girl.

Half way back to the ranch Doyle found Bert Smalling waiting for him on the road.

'If what Pellman says is true,' Smalling said, 'it means you and the Barlows are outlawed.'

'That's about the way it sizes up, Bert.'

'If I ride with you, it tars me with the same brush.'

Doyle gave him a thin smile. 'You figure to let us carry the fight alone?'

Smalling flushed. 'If Gunwright wants my

222

place, he can have it. Fighting Skull Bar is one thing. Fighting the law is another.'

'Whatever you say, Bert.'

He watched Smalling swing his horse and take a side trail. Then Doyle rode back to Cross L. He told the rest of them—the Dunkle brothers and Lew Harper—of Smalling's decision. 'How about you?' he asked.

'We'll stick,' they said.

*　　　*　　　*

The following day they got their first glimpse of the posse. Sheriff Conodine rode beside Sid Gunwright, and there were twenty men behind them. The Temple Hills Pool struck out for higher country. They were on the run and they knew it. For two days they had cold camps, not daring to risk a fire. The following day, Dave Barlow, scouting ahead, rode back to report that he had spotted three Skull Bar men driving a small herd through a canyon.

Jeb Barlow's response was fierce. 'Three of them dogs hanging by their necks won't make up for Curt, but it'll be a start.'

Doyle looked at the old man sharply, but said nothing. Throughout that morning he had been mulling over their prospects of victory. They were mighty slim, and the more he and the other ranchers were forced to run, the greater his disgust for the whole deal. At this rate they would be on the dodge for the rest of their lives. And what would it prove?

Jeb Barlow and Dave had already spurred ahead, with the Dunkle brothers and Lew Harper trailing them. Doyle had dropped behind while he tried to get a clear perspective of their problems. A sudden burst of gunfire caused him to put his horse to a gallop.

The element of surprise worked in their favor, and they caught the three Skull Bar men flat-footed. In their eagerness, Jeb and his son started firing too soon so that two of the Skull Bar men managed to get the small herd between themselves and the oncoming riders. They spun their horses and dashed back down the canyon and kept on going until they were out of sight.

But the third rider, a fat, nondescript individual on a chestnut horse, sat frozen as bullets began to kick up around him. The cattle, spooked by the firing, went crashing back down the canyon, leaving him exposed. When he finally overcame his shock and tried to turn his horse, a bullet caught it between the eyes and he was thrown heavily.

Doyle rode up to find Dave Barlow tying Tim O'Shane's hands behind his back. Old Jeb threw a noose over the fat man's head and eagerly drew it tight. O'Shane stood trembling, his eyes sick and frightened.

'We got one of 'em anyhow,' Jeb said

triumphantly. He jerked his head in the direction from which they had come. 'There's a tree up-canyon. Let's get to it.'

A sickness swept Doyle and suddenly he made up his mind. He drew his gun as Jeb turned for his horse. When Jeb Barlow saw the revolver his lined face tightened. 'What's the idea?' he demanded thinly.

'Cut him loose, Jeb,' Doyle said. Somehow just seeing Tim O'Shane there with his hands roped and a noose around his neck, brought the whole sanguinary picture into focus.

Dave Barlow stood rigid, his mustache thick and dark against his pale face. The Dunkle brothers and Lew Harper seemed undecided as to what role they should play in this. But for the moment they seemed content to let Doyle and the Barlows thrash it out.

Jeb's teeth were clenched and he yelled, 'What you trying to do, Doyle?'

'O'Shane is a forty-dollar a month cowhand,' Doyle said. 'He's not Skull Bar.'

'He's drawing their money,' Jeb Barlow said.

'Is hanging O'Shane going to finish Gunwright?' Doyle demanded, aware of a faint hope stirring in the prisoner's eyes.

Dave Barlow said, 'What did hanging Curt prove? Nothing, but they did it.' He glared at O'Shane. 'And maybe this fat one had a hand in it.'

'No—no—' O'Shane's knees started to give

225

way, but he managed to right himself. Beads of perspiration streaked his fat face, but he did not beg for mercy.

Doyle leaned over in the saddle, still gripping his gun. 'O'Shane, did you see what happened to Charlie Prince and Al Miller?'

O'Shane nodded his head, still apparently unable to find his voice.

'Will you tell the truth to Conodine?'

Again the fat man nodded his head.

Jeb sprang forward his face livid. 'You ain't cheating me of this, Doyle!' he cried, and made a play for the pistol at his belt.

Doyle rode his horse between the old man and O'Shane. 'Hold it, Jeb!'

Jeb Barlow shook his fist. He was gray about the mouth and his eyes were large and bright with anger. 'We warned Skull Bar we'd hang the first man we found in the hills! We're hanging this one, dammit!'

When Jeb Barlow tried to step around Doyle's horse, Doyle said, 'Stay away from him, Jeb. I'd hate to shoot you.'

Jeb backed up, and suddenly the pallor at the corners of his mouth deepened and spread upward. He clutched his chest, weaving a little as Dave sprang forward to steady the old man. But impatiently Jeb shrugged off his son. He glared at Doyle and shook his fist. 'Damn you—'

Suddenly his eyes rolled up in his head and his legs collapsed. He fell to the ground,

226

twitched, then lay still, his mouth open.

So quickly had it happened that at first the men were stunned. Then Dave Barlow dropped to a knee beside his father. Finally he glared up at Doyle, a terrible rage in his eyes. 'Why didn't you put a bullet in him? Pa's dead—the same as if you'd shot him!'

Doyle, still holding his gun, looked at Lew Harper. 'Cut O'Shane loose, will you, Lew? I'm going to Regency and settle this thing.'

'I'm going with you,' Harper announced, but Doyle shook his head.

'You stay here and see that Dave doesn't shoot me in the back,' Doyle said grimly.

When O'Shane was cut loose and they had given him Jeb's horse to ride, Doyle herded the unarmed man toward Regency. He rode numbly, his mind filled with the tragedy he had witnessed back in the canyon. Jeb Barlow had died hating him.

CHAPTER TWENTY-TWO

As he rode south Doyle reached one conclusion. He must finish this fight with Gunwright. If Gunwright died, the whole structure of Skull Bar's expansion into Temple Hills would collapse. As it was now, the pool could stay in the hills until they got gray-headed, but it would solve nothing.

227

They would be hounded on one side by Skull Bar and by the sheriff on the other. Yet it could all be settled swiftly, irrevocably, by the death of Sid Gunwright. Doyle had toyed with this idea earlier in the day. Now the death of Jeb and the near hanging of Tim O'Shane had crystallized his resolve.

Life suddenly had little meaning, because he knew Ellie would learn of her father's death through Dave Barlow. Dave would paint the blackest possible picture, and Ellie, try though she might to discount her hate-twisted brother's exaggerations, still would have to connect Doyle with her father's death. Thus, unspoken love might falter in the face of an ever-present reminder, draw back, and also die.

Tim O'Shane rode loosely in the saddle, the back of his shirt dark with patches of sweat, round head hanging down, as if resigned to a terrible fate.

'Feel like talking yet?' Doyle asked, as he reined in beside the fat man.

O'Shane did not look at him. 'If I talk, Gunwright will probably have me shot or hanged.'

'Back there in the hills your death wasn't a probability, it was a certainty,' Doyle reminded him.

'Yeah. And I'll remember it was you that saved my neck.'

'What about Miller and Prince?'

'They was both alive, last I heard,' O'Shane said.

Doyle looked at him in some surprise. 'But I figured Gunwright had them killed and then planned to blame it on me and the Barlows.'

'Gunwright and Fengean jumped them three Texans the night Curt Barlow was hung,' O'Shane said. He stared fearfully at the lights of Regency which were beginning to glow in the twilight shadows ahead. 'Miller and Prince hung back so's to give Tasker and the Hale woman a chance to ride for it. But Miller and Prince run out of shells and Gunwright took 'em prisoner. He had 'em taken to Skull Bar headquarters and locked up. He figured to spread the story that you and the Barlows killed them two, not letting on that both of 'em had already quit Skull Bar.'

'Keeping them prisoner would solve nothing, it seems to me.'

'Gunwright thought if anything went wrong he'd make 'em testify against you, saying you rustled Skull Bar cows.'

'You're sure about all this?'

'For a fact,' O'Shane said stoutly, recovering some of his composure. 'I was there when them Texans was made prisoner. And the rest of it I overheard when Gunwright and Fengean talked.'

'So that's the way it is.' Doyle felt a vast relief.

'But everything's changed now,' Tim O'Shane said. 'Gunwright told Fengean to turn them Texans loose and ride 'em to Canton to take the stage. They was to be warned that if they come back here, they was dead men.'

'What changed Gunwright's mind?' Doyle demanded.

'He's got you dead to rights now, Doyle. Joplin and Anse Lipscomb swear you killed Sol Dinker. And that deputy ain't been seen since the day him and Malgren and the rest of 'em went looking for you.'

Doyle digested this, then asked if Gunwright knew Malgren was dead.

'Seein's as how nobody's seen Malgren since,' O'Shane said, 'he's sure that Hamp's buried somewheres up in the Rubios.'

'That's one fact Gunwright has got straight,' Doyle said grimly.

Keeping off the main trails, Doyle took O'Shane into Regency from the west, circling around the boarded up buildings on Copperjack Street.

For a half hour after sundown it had been pitch dark, but now an early moon rose swiftly over the Temple Hills, diminishing in size as it climbed and flooding the town with silver light. Knowing he had to get information, and get it without resorting to a public place such as Pellman's, Doyle rode Tim O'Shane to the rear door of Mom

Lanfield's. Leaning over in the saddle, he rapped on the door.

In a few moments the door opened and a black-haired girl said, 'Why don't you come around front, honey?'

'Tell Mom I want to see her.'

The girl peered at him. 'You're Doyle, aren't you?'

'Yeah.'

The girl disappeared and in a moment Mom Lanfield came to the door. She wore a black comb in her dyed hair and the inevitable string of red beads. She stared suspiciously at O'Shane, then cocked an eyebrow at Doyle.

'Conodine's in town,' she said. 'He figures you're ripe for hanging.'

'Maybe. How about Gunwright? He in town?'

Mom Lanfield ignored the question. She said, 'Doris Brome come in on the afternoon stage.'

'I thought she left town with her folks,' Doyle said.

'She left town all right,' Mom Lanfield said. 'But somewhere down the line she heard about what happened to Curt Barlow and who done the dirty job. She come back. She saw Sid Gunwright standing in front of Pellman's, and by damn if that girl don't walk up to him and pull a revolver out of the pocket of her dress and say she's come to kill him.'

231

Doyle whistled under his breath. 'Did she finish the job?'

'Well, Sid never come so close to dyin' as he did that minute. But before she can pull the trigger, Clyde Fengean grabs her and takes the gun away.'

'Where's Doris now?'

'Well, in the commotion, Ellie Barlow come out of the Regency. She heard what happened and took Doris up to her room.'

'Anything else happened since I've been gone, Mom?'

'My stars, ain't that enough?' She shot O'Shane another glance. 'Ain't he working for Gunwright?'

'Not any longer,' Doyle said laconically. He tipped his hat to Mom Lanfield and urged his prisoner away from the rambling structure. They dismounted beside the two-story jail building. A light burned in the office window upstairs.

'I'm warning you, Tim,' Doyle said. 'Play it straight with Conodine—or else.'

O'Shane's fat shoulders drooped. 'I'll play your game, Doyle. I got no love for Skull Bar, after all the devilment they done.'

'Yet you kept on working for them,' Doyle reminded him.

O'Shane wiped his mouth with the back of his hand. 'You won't believe it, but when me and them two fellas got that herd to Harvey Brome's old place today, I figured to keep right on going. I'd have run out before, but was afraid Gunwright would have me shot.' He sighed. 'Now it don't matter.'

Two figures at the big window of the jail office caught Doyle's eye—Joplin talking to Sheriff Conodine. He shoved O'Shane into the shadows against the jail wall as they heard someone coming down the stone steps. In a moment the lank Joplin appeared, looked warily around, then started down the street. Doyle waited until he saw the deputy enter Pellman's. Then he drew his gun and started to climb the stairs with O'Shane.

Conodine was sitting before his desk, staring at some papers, when the two men came up behind him. Hearing the scuff of their boots on the floor, he turned. His face went white.

'Don't make a move,' Doyle said, and motioned for O'Shane to step over beside the desk.

'I knew you were a man with nerve, Doyle,' Conodine said thinly. 'But I didn't think you had guts enough to put a gun on me in my own jail.'

'You know it now,' Doyle said.

The sheriff had one of Gunwright's cigars clamped in his teeth. He looked not only angered but wary of what might follow this bold invasion of his Regency headquarters. Doyle knew it was possible that Conodine had been promised a financial reward from

Gunwright if this grim business turned out to the advantage of Skull Bar.

'You're after the Pool because they're accused of killing Al Miller and Charlie Prince,' Doyle said.

'I don't know about the Pool,' Conodine said heavily. 'But I'm after you and the Barlows for it.'

'Is that the only charge against us?'

Conodine looked at O'Shane, then at Doyle. 'Isn't that enough?'

'Tell him, Tim,' Doyle said. 'What happened to Miller and Prince?'

For a moment the fat O'Shane floundered. Then he plunged into it. He kept going, sick and perspiring, until the story was told.

'Them two Texans was herded off to Skull Bar,' he wound up. 'So far as I know they're still there.'

'That doesn't make sense,' Conodine snapped, biting down on his cigar. 'Why would Gunwright take them prisoner?'

'Sheriff, if you swallowed the story about Doyle and the Barlows 'gulching Miller and Prince, then them two was to be taken out somewheres and shot.'

Conodine winced at the reference to his gullibility.

'But now with this Sol Dinker business,' O'Shane went on, 'Gunwright figures to either have Miller and Prince testify against Doyle or run 'em out of the country.'

234

Conodine seemed to shrink into his chair. 'Why in hell did I ever get into this?'

'You wanted the job,' Doyle reminded him, 'or you'd never have run for office.'

Conodine glared at him, then threw his cigar to the floor. 'I've played Gunwright's game because he has political connections. He and the governor are—' He lifted his hands, let them fall. 'Well, no matter about that.' He clenched his hands. 'Harvey Brome's daughter tried to kill Gunwright tonight. I could hold her on an assault charge, but Gunwright has refused to sign a complaint.'

'That's the same as admitting he hanged Curt Barlow,' Doyle said.

'I know it. And that's what worries me. Gunwright claims some of his men found Curt with a running iron. He swears he had nothing to do with the hanging. Yet he won't have the woman arrested who tried to murder him.'

'Get Gunwright up here,' Doyle told the harassed sheriff. 'Let him face O'Shane. You can tell quick enough which one is lying. Then send a posse to Skull Bar. If Miller and Prince are still around you'll—'

Conodine lurched to his feet. 'I believe O'Shane's story. I don't know why. I just do. But I can tell you this, Doyle—one witness isn't enough. You've got to get another who saw Gunwright jump them that night.'

Doyle thought swiftly. 'Sabrina Hale.

You'd take her word?'

Conodine scowled. 'Is she likely to turn against Gunwright? I hear they're going to be married.'

'It all ended the night Curt Barlow was hanged. Sabrina saw the whole thing.'

Conodine's mouth fell open. 'The hell you say. Pretty gruesome thing for a woman to watch.'

Doyle gave the sheriff a hard smile. 'I think Sabrina will be on our side.'

Conodine rubbed his jaw. 'There's another thing, Doyle.' He started for a small storage room off the office. 'Some papers I want you to see.'

Doyle followed him on tip toe. He rammed his gun against the sheriff's back just as Conodine gingerly lifted a sawed-off shotgun from a wall rack. The sheriff put the gun back and sighed mournfully.

Doyle backed up so he could keep an eye on O'Shane. 'Why the change of heart, Sheriff? I thought I had you convinced.'

'You did—up to a point.'

'And that point?'

'What happened to Sol Dinker?' Conodine demanded. 'I hear you killed him when he tried to arrest you.'

Doyle said, 'One thing at a time, Sheriff. I'm going to have to trust you whether I like it or not. But I believe you're honest. Maybe foolish, but honest.'

Conodine's mouth jerked. 'I don't take being called a fool—'

'I'd advise you to hunt up Joplin and put him in a cell,' Doyle cut in crisply. 'He and Dinker were working for Gunwright.'

Conodine blinked and swallowed. 'Can you prove that?'

'Not now, maybe, but I will before this is over.' He and the sheriff went back into the office where O'Shane stood, flabbily weary, beside the desk. 'I haven't anything against you Conodine, except your judgment in picking deputies.'

Conodine stared down at the littered desk. 'I've been wondering about that myself lately. I began to lose faith in Gunwright when he refused to fire Malgren after that unfortunate episode with the Barlow girl.' He cleared his throat. 'Malgren's dead, isn't he?'

'Yes.'

'One thing you've done, Doyle, I approve of.' He slanted a look at O'Shane. 'Mind being locked up for a while? It's for your own good. If Skull Bar gets wind of what you plan to do, you won't live long.'

'I don't have much choice,' O'Shane said.

Frowning, the sheriff took a ring of keys from a peg over his desk. 'I'll go along with you, Doyle, for the present. But I still want an accounting for Dinker.'

'You'll get it. Either Joplin or Anse Lipscomb will give you the truth of what happened that day.'

'At the end of a gun?' Conodine said bluntly.

'Fear of death is the only way scum like that will talk,' Doyle told him.

'You go get the Hale woman. I'll find Joplin.'

Doyle went downstairs, not at all certain he could fully trust Conodine. The man had seemed genuinely disturbed by O'Shane's recital of what had really taken place the night Prince and Miller disappeared, but he knew it was within Conodine's power to shoot O'Shane and start yelling for Skull Bar. Still, Doyle knew, he had to gamble. This was it. If Conodine had his hand in Gunwright's pocket, then all his plans would avail him little. But of one thing he was certain. He would not leave Regency until Gunwright was dead.

CHAPTER TWENTY-THREE

An ominous quiet hung over Regency, as if the town breathlessly awaited the coming of a storm. Doyle rode cautiously across weed-grown lots, past abandoned shacks until he came to the rear of Sabrina's yellow house. Through the leafing trees he could see not a single window aglow with lamplight. He felt disappointed. Leaving his buckskin out of sight in the trees, near the road, he advanced through the silvered moonlight that made the yard a perfect place for an ambush. If Gunwright had Skull Bar men planted here or in the house, they could easily cut him down. And Gunwright might very well figure that, for romantic or other reasons, Doyle would sooner or later pay the big yellow house a visit.

As he crossed the yard the stillness seemed to press down on him. Not even the sound of the piano from Mom Lanfield's. Was it possible, he asked himself, that Sabrina had overcome her revulsion at seeing Curt Barlow hanged and gone to Skull Bar with Gunwright?

Keeping to the shadows of the big carriage house, Doyle halted, studying the rear entrance of the main house. There was no movement. He started forward.

'Doyle.'

A trapped feeling engulfed Doyle. He spun, realizing the voice belonged to Pete Tasker. His gun was out, cocked, but the tall, red-haired Texan had made no move toward his own revolver. The last time they had been together with the night at Cross L when Doyle slapped Sabrina.

'Sabrina's in here,' Tasker whispered, jerking a thumb at the carriage house. When Doyle hesitated, the Texan said grimly, 'I'd have joined your bunch when Al and Charlie got theirs, but I was scared to leave Sabrina alone.'

'Then you don't believe the story that the Barlows and me killed them.'

'Hell no.'

Doyle allowed a tight grin to touch his lips and told the Texan that so far as he knew his two partners were prisoners at Skull Bar. At the worst they had been herded to Canton and there placed on a stage at gunpoint with the warning not to come back.

Doyle followed Tasker into the carriage house. Mingled with the odors of hay and leather he caught Sabrina's familiar scent. Tasker lighted a lantern and the glow revealed Sabrina. She stood rigid, hands clenched into fists. She wore the same mud-splattered black riding habit that had been her attire the night she saw Curt Barlow hanged.

'Hello, Kermit,' she said in a dead voice, making no move to go to him. 'I convinced Pete that I deserved the slap you gave me at Cross L. It brought me to my senses, I guess.'

Doyle looked around the big barnlike structure. Two horses moved restlessly in stalls. A pair of buggies, their shafts tied back, had been wheeled to the rear of the carriage house. In the center of the runway, straw had been piled on the ground and covered with blankets. There were two

240

pillows.

When she saw Doyle staring at the makeshift bed, Sabrina's face flushed. 'Will you leave us alone a minute, Pete?' she asked the Texan.

Without a word, Pete Tasker stepped outside and closed the door behind him.

Doyle watched Sabrina lower herself to a bale of hay, her movements graceful even under her stress. In her dark hair were bits of straw, and under her eyes, circles of weariness. It was the first time he had ever seen her when she was not dressed for the eye of man or woman alike.

'I knew I had lost you that night at the Cross L, Kermit.' She spoke without her customary bitterness when plans had not gone as she expected. 'I saw the way you looked at Ellie Barlow.' She studied his face in the lantern light. 'You love her, don't you?'

'Yes. But nothing will come of it. Her father died—because of me.'

Sabrina's shoulders moved. 'Whatever love you had for me is gone. I know that. I turned back to you too late, Kermit.' She laughed harshly, and the sound was unbecoming to one so regal. 'I think I've finally found my own level.'

'Tasker?'

'He saved my life. If Sid could have caught me that night, I believe he would have shot me.' She gave him a tight smile. 'Pete got food from the big house and we've been staying here together. Sid thinks I've left town.' She rose and walked over to the blankets and with the toe of her shoe turned one of them back. 'Texans have odd ideas about their women. He says we'll have to get married now.'

Doyle had holstered his gun and now he built a cigarette, trying to put from his mind even pity for this woman he once had loved. 'You're going to marry Tasker?'

'Why not? He's never been to San Francisco. And he likes the idea. I won't be able to live as I planned, but what money I have left will give us a start.' She smiled, a little wistfully, he thought. 'Maybe I can make a gentleman out of Pete. I'm going to try.'

Doyle started to say something, but remained silent. At the moment he suddenly felt sorry for Pete Tasker. One day the man would long for a saddle under him and the feel of the wind in his face. Then Sabrina would be alone in San Francisco. Perhaps it would be better that way.

Stepping to the door, he called Tasker inside. Then he explained his plan to Sabrina. 'If I bring the sheriff here, will you tell him it was Skull Bar that tried to ride you and Pete down the night Charlie and Al were taken prisoner?'

'If it will help finish Sid, I'll do it,' she said

vehemently, and Tasker gripped her arm and grinned.

'And, Pete, you'll tell the sheriff that you and your friends had already quit Skull Bar and were riding for me?'

'Hell, yes,' Pete Tasker said, and apologized to Sabrina for swearing.

Doyle thought wryly, Sabrina, you won't have to make a gentleman out of him. He's already more of a one than Gunwright—or me.

Tasker wanted to go with Doyle, but Doyle shook his head. 'You stay here with Sabrina,' he said. 'She's not safe alone until Sid Gunwright is through.'

Then he left and rode his buckskin along the desolate street known as Copperjack. An era had ended for Regency when copper stocks declined. Another era would end if Sid Gunwright died this night. In the alley behind Pellman's he left his horse and stepped through the rear door. He moved along a corridor, past the big, deserted 'family room.' From a curtained doorway he studied the crowded barroom.

But instead of lining up at the bar or occupying the gaming tables, the men were ringed about something on the floor. Doyle felt a tightening in the pit of his stomach. He saw Loren Pellman hurrying from his bar with a pail of water and a clean rag. And at that moment Pellman saw Doyle's beckoning finger and a corner of his face in the curtained doorway. The fat saloonman stiffened, shoved water bucket and cloths to one of his patrons and wheeled for the corridor.

'What's up?' Doyle demanded.

'Conodine,' Pellman whispered. 'They found him laying in the alley with his head nearly beat off. They'd have finished him, but a mule skinner and his swamper surprised 'em and they run off.'

Pellman paused. Doyle wiped a shaking hand across his eyes and breathed deeply.

'Is Conodine dead?' he asked at last.

'No, but he's unconscious. Joplin says you done it, Kermit.'

Somehow Doyle regained self control. Then, quickly, he sketched for Pellman what had happened at the jail between himself and Conodine. Hearing a familiar voice, Doyle turned and saw the lanky, tobacco-chewing Joplin in the barroom. He was talking to some of the men and gesturing toward Conodine on the floor. There was worry on the deputy's long face, and Doyle took hope from this. In a moment Joplin headed for the front door.

'Keep Conodine here,' Doyle told Pellman grimly. 'If you don't put a guard around him, they'll finish the job.'

'You can't stay in town, Kermit. They'll gun you sure. Sid and Fengean are here.'

'Any of the Skull Bar bunch with them?'

244

'I dunno. But for God's sake watch yourself, Kermit.'

'You watch Conodine,' Doyle warned. 'That's the main thing.'

'I'll get Link Johnson,' Pellman said. 'If anybody tries to fix the sheriff, they'll get a hole in the head.'

When Pellman returned to the barroom, Doyle saw him draw the hardware merchant aside and whisper a few words. Then the tall Johnson followed Pellman to the bar. There the saloonman pressed a sawed-off shotgun into his hands.

Satisfied, Doyle left by the alley door, and started looking for Tom Joplin.

*　　*　　*

Sid Gunwright put a hip on the porch rail of the Regency, keeping to the deepest shadows. There were few men on the streets tonight, he observed, and in the quiet which lay over the town he sensed the brooding presence of Fate, the blind judge. It was the same as cutting for high card. You won or lost on the turn of a card. If Sheriff Conodine died, you won; if he lived, the game was up.

Thus far, his worst error had been in allowing Fengean and Joplin to handle important assignments. But how was he to know they would botch everything? He glared through the darkness at them. There they stood, an elbow's length away, discussing the possibilities of another try at the sheriff. Fools.

And this afternoon, to see that pretty Doris Brome step off the stage and cross the street toward him ... And she'd been smiling, Gunwright recalled. He had thought then that she was much better looking than he remembered; the beaten down look she seemed to share with her father was oddly missing.

She'd had her right hand buried in the pocket of her dress. She'd stepped up to him and pulled that revolver, that funny little nickel-plated affair. He remembered how his throat had suddenly gone dry. And by shutting his eyes he could remember the cold fury on her face and the words she had hurled at him.

'You hanged Curt! You murdered him—'

And if Fengean hadn't come along the walk and grabbed the girl, the gun would have put a piece of lead in his vitals. It was a disquieting thought.

After Ellie Barlow had taken the girl into the hotel, the true damage of the situation was easily ascertained. Half the town had heard Doris Brome's accusation and those who had not been present had learned it later. Men had a way of looking at him now. Not open defiance, but a studied ignoring of his presence.

Because his inner rage needed venting, Gunwright turned on Joplin. 'Why was I ever fool enough to buy your badge?'

Joplin licked his lips. 'Don't blame me, Sid. Conodine called me into the alley behind Pellman's. What could I do? I went back there, and he told me O'Shane was ready to talk. Then he accused me and Dinker of working for you.'

Fengean started to light his pipe, then thought better of it. 'You've got to understand this, Sid. Joplin gave me the nod, and I trailed him and the sheriff to the alley. I heard what Conodine said.' He shrugged. 'The sheriff has a thick skull. That's all you can say about it. I tried hard enough.'

'He'd be dead,' Joplin put in nervously, 'if that freight outfit hadn't come along the alley when it did. Of all the luck.'

'Did they see you?' Gunwright demanded.

Joplin shrugged. 'I blamed Conodine's busted head on Kermit Doyle. Ain't anybody stepped up to claim different. No, I reckon they didn't see us.'

Fengean clicked the stem of his pipe against his teeth. 'Now I'd go along with knocking Conodine out until maybe you could get him out to the ranch and talk sense to him. But killing him is—'

'No matter,' Gunwright snapped, unable to conceal his venom. 'You bungled it. Both of you!'

Fengean flipped a hand across his short beard and laughed. 'I'd say it was bungled a long time ago, Sid.'

'Just how long ago?' Gunwright asked thinly.

'It started with hanging Curt Barlow. That was a fool play.'

Gunwright gave the short-legged Fengean a cold stare. 'Sounds like you've taken out membership in the Temple Hills Pool.'

Fengean shook his head. 'I'm still for Skull Bar even if I do think you went a little loco.' He sighed. 'You got Harvey Brome's place legally. You should've been satisfied.'

Gunwright slid off the porch rail, hating the foreman. 'I wish I had Hamp Malgren. He was crazy in the head maybe, but he had more guts than the whole crew put together.'

For a long while Fengean just stared up at his employer. Then he said quietly, 'I'm glad to hear you think Hamp Malgren was a better man than I am. That's the final insult, Sid.' He turned on his heel and started across the porch.

At that moment Lew Gorling, his arm still in a sling, came racing up the steps. He caught the Skull Bar foreman by the arm. 'I just seen Sabrina Hale,' he said breathlessly. 'Her and Pete Tasker has been holing up in the carriage house. Anse Lipscomb is watching to see they don't pull out—'

Fengean shook his hand off. 'Don't tell me.

I'm not working for Skull Bar no more.'

But Gunwright came up quickly, shoving the yellow-haired Gorling aside. 'Don't quit me now, Clyde. I'm sorry. You're worth more than a hundred Hamp Malgrens.'

Gorling scratched his head, mystified as to what had brought about this rupture between the boss and his foreman.

'I don't know, Sid,' Fengean said.

'For the old man, then, if not for me. My dad trusted you. You were one of his best friends—'

Fengean took a moment to stare across the flat-roofed buildings towards the distant Rubios. 'All right,' he said. 'For the old man.' He turned and regarded Gunwright solemnly. 'God help us, Sid, if this night's business works out bad. You'll leave Regency with a whole lot less than your old man had the day he come here.'

Gunwright said, 'Thanks, Clyde.' And then, as if he had just surmounted one crisis, the old arrogance crept back into his voice as he turned to Gorling. 'Are Sabrina and Tasker alone?'

'Yeah. I was riding down Copperjack Street when I seen the side door open,' Gorling said. 'Doyle come out. He got away in the dark before I could get him. But I sneaked up at the carriage house and heard the Hale woman and Tasker talking. Anse Lipscomb is watching 'em.'

Gunwright fingered his chin and looked at Joplin. 'If Pellman's should catch on fire the crowd might stampede and leave Conodine behind. At any rate, in the confusion I imagine the job you started on him could be finished.' He jerked a thumb at Gorling. 'You go with him.'

Gorling hesitated. 'What if the whole town burns?'

'That would be most unfortunate,' Gunwright said. 'Come on, Clyde.'

CHAPTER TWENTY-FOUR

Halfway down the alley Doyle suddenly remembered Tim O'Shane and decided to abandon his search for Joplin. With Conodine injured, he reasoned, there was nothing to prevent Joplin or some of the Skull Bar crowd from silencing the fat man. He turned quickly and crossed a vacant lot. A moment's study of the jail office showed no sign of movement inside. But he couldn't be sure. Cautiously, gun in hand, he began to climb the stone stairs leading to the second floor.

The office door stood open, the lamp still burned on the sheriff's desk. On the wall were the keys. Taking these, Doyle started down the corridor that led to the cells. But he heard a footstep on the stairs. He flattened against the wall just as a mustached man peered into the office, saw it was empty and stepped in. It was Dave Barlow and he held a gun.

Doyle said from the corridor, 'You're covered, Dave. Drop it.'

Dave Barlow spun, looking down the corridor. 'That you, Doyle?' he called.

Doyle moved into the office as Ellie stepped up behind her brother. She rushed across the office and flung herself into his arms. Stiffly Doyle held her, letting down the hammer of his revolver.

He looked across her shoulder and saw Doris Brome in the doorway and he knew she had come here with the Barlows.

Doyle stroked Ellie's hair. 'You know about your father?' he asked.

She nodded, sniffing back tears. 'Dave told me. But it wasn't your fault. You were right not to hang that man. Two wrongs don't make a right.' She made a hopeless gesture. 'Dad's heart was bad for a long time. His terrible temper killed him, Kermit, not you.'

'How do you feel about it, Dave?' Doyle asked.

'I dunno,' he muttered, scowling down at the stone floor of the jail office.

'He'll change,' Ellie said. She still wore Doyle's wool shirt, the sleeves rolled up, and her denim pants. She carried a carbine. Ellie smiled up at Doyle. 'Doris is going to stay with me for a while. She doesn't want to go with her folks. This is home to her.'

Doris Brome's underlip began to tremble. She was dressed for traveling, her brown hair neatly coiled; and he wondered at the nerve of this girl who would carry a revolver in the pocket of her gray dress and step up with it to a man like Gunwright.

Doris swayed a little and Dave put a thick arm around her waist to steady her. 'She loved Curt,' he said. 'Maybe I can be like a brother to her for a time.' Dave spoke awkwardly and his face was flushed. 'Maybe later on I can be something else to her—'

Doris made no reply, but she did move closer into the circle of his arm.

Then Ellie gripped Doyle by the wrists. 'The Pool didn't desert you, Kermit. They're here.' Quickly she recounted how Lew Harper had talked the Dunkle brothers into riding to Regency, persuading them it was their fight. On the outskirts of town they had run into the old cook, Skip Harlow with the 'boss wagon' and five Skull Bar men. They were camping, awaiting Gunwright's signal to ride with him to a gathering grounds where the whole Skull Bar calf crop was to be shoved into the Temple Hills. 'Harper and the Dunkle boys are out there holding those men prisoner,' she said. 'Dave came to the hotel to see if I was all right.'

Dave, still with his arm about Doris

252

Brome's waist, said, 'We left the hotel by the back door and just then I seen you crossing to the jail here.'

Ellie's grip tightened on Doyle's wrists. 'It's all over, Kermit. Conodine has regained consciousness, so I hear. He was badly beaten.'

'Yes, I know.' Even this news could not thrill him. As long as Gunwright still lived the thing could not be over.

'The sheriff is going to arrest Gunwright—'

The double blast of a shotgun roared through the town. A man screamed horribly.

Throwing the ring of cell keys at Dave Barlow, Doyle yelled for him to release Tim O'Shane. Then he sprinted down the stairs, with Ellie crying for him to come back.

*   *   *

Link Johnson had lived thirteen years in Regency without distinguishing himself beyond the routine of furnishing the citizenry with implements of peace and war from the shelves of his hardware store. But this night the fleshless, gray merchant, holding a double-barreled shotgun, had a feeling of greatness, of contributing something to the welfare of this town where he had lived so long.

This was a momentous night. Sheriff Conodine, bloodied at the head but clear of

253

eye, was sitting up on a poker table. 'It was Fengean that struck me down,' he said to the crowd in the barroom. 'Him and my deputy, Joplin.'

With the shotgun under one arm, Johnson took the empty water pail Pellman handed him and stepped out the rear door to pump it full. Pellman had said he wanted fresh water with which to bathe the sheriff's head again.

It was when Johnson reached the alley that a strong odor of kerosene came to his nostrils. He peered to his left, instantly apprehensive. Surprised, he saw Joplin and Lew Gorling in the clear moonlight slopping the contents of two kerosene tins over the rear wall of Pellman's. Johnson's sudden appearance had startled the two men, and now the three of them stood stiffly as if not knowing what to do next.

It was the deputy, Tom Joplin, who yelled for Gorling to get out of the way and drew his gun.

But Link Johnson acted instinctively. He dropped the empty water bucket and shifted the shotgun all in the same movement. He could see both faces clearly, Joplin's long and narrow, white with fury, the jaws moving on the inevitable chew of tobacco. Lew Gorling's bandaged arm was another spot of white.

Johnson tripped both barrels and the recoil knocked him back against the wall.

Joplin lay with the kerosene can under

him, dead from the full blast of the lethal weapon which had shattered his upper body. Lew Gorling, at the fringe of the target, had taken enough buckshot to wound but not kill. He tried to crawl away, but collapsed. He began to scream and kept on screaming.

Suddenly the alley filled with men, and Kermit Doyle was shoving his way through the crowd, gripping a revolver. Seeing that Joplin was dead, he bent over Gorling.

'Where's Gunwright?' Doyle demanded.

Gorling began to laugh wildly. 'You turned them horses on Slim.' He had raised himself to his elbows and fell back. 'Go to hell, Doyle.'

Doyle rose to see Pellman at his elbow. 'Some of your hill friends just brought in a bunch of Skull Bar riders with their hands in the air,' Pellman said.

Doyle did not reply. He heard the creaking of a heavy vehicle, and through the slot between the buildings, he saw the Skull Bar 'boss wagon,' the six mule team driven by the gray-haired cook, Skip Harlow, moving down the main street under the rifle of Lew Harper.

Doyle looked down at Gorling, bleeding from half a dozen wounds. 'I felt as bad about Slim Dorn as you did,' he told the yellow-haired Skull Bar man. 'Slim would be alive today if Gunwright hadn't made you boys trespass on my property. What would you have done, in my place? Knuckle under

You know damn well you wouldn't. If anybody's to blame for Slim's death it's Gunwright.' Doyle waited a moment, while the crowd watched tensely, and then he said, 'Where did Gunwright go?'

'To the Hale house.'

Doyle sprinted along the alley toward the main street. Catching up the first saddler at the Pellman rail, he spurred to the east end of town. As he drew closer, he felt his heart lurch, for through the poplars he could see a shaft of yellow light. That meant the door to the carriage house stood wide open.

At the picket fence, he caught a glimpse of Anse Lipscomb's heavy figure. Lipscomb saw him and tried to lift a gun, but Doyle rode him down. The horse's shoulder knocked the stableman sprawling into the street, and the shooting started as Doyle sent the horse over the picket fence. He saw the bright orange streaks of flame. In the carriage house doorway stood Pete Tasker, firing at someone in the yard. As Doyle's horse struck the ground on four legs, Tasker crumpled.

The Texan yelled, 'Sabrina—smash the lantern!' Then his voice died.

Firing increased and suddenly, straight ahead, Doyle saw the Skull Bar foreman with the heavy torso and the incredibly short legs. Clyde Fengean stepped from his shelter in the trees and turned his gun. The muzzle winked Doyle.

256

The blow was savage. It swept Doyle from the saddle. But when he struck the ground and rolled to a sitting position he still held his gun. A terrible pain high up told him that the bullet from Fengean's gun probably had smashed his collarbone, and he could feel the sticky warmth of blood on his flesh. He saw Fengean running toward him.

'Who's out there?' Fengean called, and Doyle realized then that he was sitting in a pool of deep shadow. The Skull Bar foreman couldn't tell whom he had shot.

Fengean slowed his pace, peering forward, and Doyle could see that he clutched the stem of the old pipe in his teeth. Doyle's horse was bucking along the fence, setting up a racket. Fengean turned to look that way, and Doyle managed to get to one knee. From the corner of his eye Fengean caught the movement and pivoted. Doyle aimed for the thickest part of that thick body and fired.

The foreman sighed, 'Ah-h-h-h,' and fired his revolver into the ground and doubled up almost at Doyle's feet.

Doyle rose, the movement tearing at him. He found it difficult to breathe. He kicked Fengean's gun away.

The foreman lifted his head. 'Gunwright—he's gone after the girl—I hope you get him—'

At a crooked run, Doyle started for the carriage house, bent over as pain swarmed along his torn muscles and nerves. Behind him, in the street, he heard horses and the shouting of men.

Ahead, lamplight still spilled out the carriage house doorway and over Pete Tasker's body.

When he reached the carriage house he heard Gunwright say calmly, 'Come in, Doyle.'

Looking in, he saw Sid Gunwright holding the muzzle of a cocked revolver at Sabrina's temple. The rancher stood behind her, his left arm around her waist so that she was drawn up tightly against him. He had lost his hat, and perspiration glistened on his face.

Doyle started for the doorway, his gun suddenly an impossible weight in his hand. He stepped over the red-haired Pete Tasker.

Sabrina's eyes were glassy with fear, her lips a bloodless line across her white face. 'Kill him, Kermit,' she whispered hoarsely. 'Kill him.'

Doyle waited, feeling the urge to be sick. The wetness increased across his shirt, and he sagged lower in the doorway. But from the corners of his eyes he watched Gunwright's face. Gunwright said, 'Tell me something, Doyle.'

'What?' Doyle gasped, and very slowly he started to lift his gun, turning his body so that Gunwright could not see the movement.

Gunwright went on smoothly, and Doyle

knew it would be only a moment before the rancher killed him: 'You really did drink a bottle of beer in Sabrina's kitchen that day—'

Sabrina sagged. The weight momentarily pulled Gunwright off balance. Then she was flinging herself to the floor, slipping from under his heavy arm.

Whether it was because the Skull Bar man considered his enemy too far gone or because Sabrina's sudden action threw him off, Doyle never knew. All he could think of was one shot. Just one—and quickly. In the instant Gunwright was exposed, Doyle aimed for the ruby stickpin in the front of the man's shirt. He kept on firing until his gun was empty.

Pete Tasker, lying in the doorway, lifted his head and murmured, 'You got him, Doyle,' and fainted again.

The yard and the carriage house swarmed with men. They clustered around Doyle and the dead Gunwright. And then Doyle saw the Skull Bar 'boss wagon' pull into the yard. Skip Harlow climbed stiffly down from the seat and unlocked the door. He went inside and came out again with a blanket. 'Some of you boys help me carry the boss?' the old cook asked. 'I'm takin' him home.'

'I always had the idea you hated Gunwright,' one of the men said.

'Reckon,' Skip Harlow said. 'But the old man would want it this way. I'm doin' it for him.'

Doyle observed this, standing with his back to an aspen. Somebody had given him a bottle. He took a drink, but the pain was still there. His head felt strange, unlike his own. He saw Sabrina standing tall and straight, her dark hair loose about her face and shoulders.

Somebody had turned Pete Tasker over on his back. He was shot high in the chest, but Texans were tough.

'He'll pull out of it,' Doyle told Sabrina, aware that his voice was fading. 'You'll live in Frisco, after all.'

Sabrina said, her lips barely moving, 'I wonder if I care very much.' She looked at Doyle, then walked to where Pete Tasker lay and dropped to her knees.

With the men staring anxiously at him, Doyle took a step back into the yard. He saw Ellie Barlow running toward him. Just as his knees buckled, he thought, There's always another dream and a better one.

Photoset, printed and bound in Great Britain by REDWOOD PRESS LIMITED, Melksham, Wiltshire